"Fiona, I didn't expe

As her eyes adjusted to the [...]
Meredith and offered her a smile. Ian sat some distance away,
and if she didn't know better, Fiona would think her brother
was royally irritated.

"Dear," Ian said, "why don't you introduce Fiona to our
guest?"

Meredith looked flustered. A woman—the one she thought
was Violet—dressed in a traveling suit of fine navy wool and
matching hat sat across the table from her. The woman's face
beamed, and her smile revealed perfect teeth framed by full,
red lips.

"I'm Elizabeth," the elegant woman said. "Elizabeth Bentley."

"This is my sister, Fiona," Ian supplied.

Elizabeth reached out to place a gloved hand atop Meredith's.
"I want to thank you for your letter. I must say I never expected
to hear from you." She paused. "From either of you, actually."

"Yes, well, about that letter." Meredith swallowed hard and
cast a furtive glance at Fiona. "You see, that letter was written
months ago. Ages, actually. I thought that Tucker—"

"Thought Tucker what?"

Fiona turned to see her soon-to-be husband standing in
the door. She offered him a smile, but he looked right past
her. "Tucker?"

No response. She tried again as he stepped into a shaft of
daylight. Still he did not respond.

What Fiona saw on his face, however, frightened her. In
the span of half a second, the man she loved had completely
forgotten she was in the room.

KATHLEEN Y'BARBO is a tenth-generation Texan and mother of three grown sons and a teenage daughter. She is a graduate of Texas A&M University and an award-winning novelist of Christian and young adult fiction. Kathleen is a former treasurer for the American Christian Fiction Writers and is a member of Inspirational Writers Alive, Words for the Journey, and The Authors Guild. Find out more about Kathleen at www.kathleenybarbo.com.

Books by Kathleen Y'Barbo

Golden Twilight

Kathleen Y'Barbo

Heartsong Presents

To Cathy and Kelly Hake, who prayed me through this one, and to Mary Connealy, whose dream of writing about Alaska gave birth to the stories and characters that became the Alaska Brides series. Also, I am deeply indebted to Karl Gurcke, historian of the Klondike Gold Rush National Historical Park in Skagway, Alaska, for his insights into the rich history of the area around which the fictional town of Goose Chase is set.

A note from the Author:
I love to hear from my readers! You may correspond with me by writing:

Kathleen Y'Barbo
Author Relations
PO Box 721
Uhrichsville, OH 44683

ISBN 978-1-59789-391-6

GOLDEN TWILIGHT

All scripture quotations are taken from the King James Version of the Bible.

All of the characters and events in this book are fictitious. Any resemblance to actual persons, living or dead, or to actual events is purely coincidental.

Our mission is to publish and distribute inspirational products offering exceptional value and biblical encouragement to the masses.

PRINTED IN THE U.S.A.

one

April 23, 1899, Oregon

As far back as she could remember, Fiona Rafferty wanted to be a doctor. While other girls her age were cutting paper dolls from the Sears Roebuck catalog, she spent her time patching up ornery barn cats and setting bird wings—when she wasn't fishing with Da. By the summer of her tenth year, she'd even saved the life of her father's prized spaniel after the old gray mare kicked him.

Her brothers, Braden and Ian, told her she had a talent for healing. If only that talent hadn't failed her the one time it mattered most. With the proper training, Fiona had no doubt she could have saved Ma.

Fiona shrugged off the memory of her mother's illness and forced the feather duster to continue its path down the spines of the books in Da's library. For a man who made his living from the earth, her father was an educated man. He'd mortgaged his dreams to buy this farm, only to see the love of his life buried beneath the uncompromising Oregon dirt.

From nothing, John Rafferty had made a life for his family. Surely he would understand her need to do the same. To make her own life.

Even as she entertained the thought, she knew better. With Ma gone, the only reaction Da had when Fiona broached the topic of medical school was a frown and a swift change of subject.

She heard the door open and close. Da was home for lunch. Smoothing her hair back from her face, Fiona dropped the feather duster beside the bookcase and scurried to the kitchen to prepare the table.

Today, he would have his favorite, a thick beef stew with carrots and potatoes. Fiona had outdone herself with the corn bread she'd whipped up, and she made sure fresh butter sat at the ready. Da did love his corn bread with ample butter.

Along with the meal, Fiona planned to serve up a side dish of careful conversation. She patted the pocket of her apron and smiled. The letter had finally come, and she would soon be going away to study medicine. All that remained was to break the news to Da.

Fiona headed for the dining room but stopped short when she heard a second male voice. The words were soft, a murmur almost, but she distinctly heard her name mentioned in the same sentence with "Alaska."

She drew in a breath and let it out slowly. Surely Da had told the visitor of his sons and daughters-in-law who lived in the North Country, then made mention of his remaining younger daughter. "Yes, that's it," Fiona said.

Touching the letter in her pocket one last time, she fashioned a smile and stepped into the dining room. Soon his remaining daughter would leave, as well, but not for Alaska.

"Ah, there's Fiona now." Da rose, as did the man sitting across from him. A woman of plain countenance and plainer dress remained seated at the stranger's side. "Welcome our guests, daughter. Rev. and Mrs. Minter, may I present my daughter, Fiona?"

"Pleased, I'm sure, Miss Rafferty," the reverend said.

"The Minters are headed to Alaska to start a church among the miners at Skagway," Da continued.

"And from what we've heard, we'll be working with some independent characters," the Reverend Minter added. "Your father said your brothers are up that way. Maybe they've written to you about how many of the locals are protesting the U.S. Post Office changing the name of their town from *Skaguay* to *Skagway*. Can't see as how it makes that much difference, but even the local newspaper refuses to change the spelling of the name. In any event, we hope to contact your brothers and send back word of their welfare."

"And don't you forget to hug my new grandson." Da patted the letter he'd carried with him since its arrival some two weeks ago. "I have it on good authority that Douglas Rafferty is a fine and healthy boy, not that we Raffertys would have anything less."

The men shared a laugh while the pastor's wife unabashedly studied Fiona. When Fiona met the woman's pointed stare, she was greeted with a smirk.

"Fetch extra plates, daughter," her father said. "We men are famished."

Fiona quickly rejected Mrs. Minter's offer of help and bustled off to the kitchen to retrieve the necessary plates and utensils. Because of the unexpected guests, the corn bread would all be eaten with the noon meal, leaving none to mix in a glass of sweet milk for Da's bedtime snack.

The kitchen door opened, and the pastor's wife stepped in. "Are you sure you don't need any help?"

"Oh no," Fiona said. "Da would tan my hide if I put guests to work. My ma raised me better than that."

The woman nodded and stepped back to let the door shut, but not before she gave Fiona a look that said she doubted the statement.

"Humph," Fiona whispered. "I sure hope they don't plan on spending the night."

Fiona returned to the dining room to see the guests were made welcome, then proceeded to serve the meal. Finally, she joined them, sitting at the opposite end of the long table from her father, who offered a genuine smile before returning to his chat with the Reverend and Mrs. Minter.

When the pleasantries had been dispensed with, Da said grace. As Fiona lifted her head, she noticed the reverend's wife staring again. Their gazes met, and Mrs. Minter quickly looked away, but not before Fiona detected something in the woman's gray eyes.

Pity.

Fiona sucked in a deep breath. Why would a mouse of a woman feel sorry for her?

"Your father tells me you're quite a seamstress," the reverend said.

"Actually, I'm not really a—"

"Indeed she is," Da interjected. "Her mother made certain Fiona was adept at all the womanly arts." He paused. "Rest her precious soul," he added in a near whisper.

"She's in a much better place," the reverend said. "One where there is no death or illness."

Mrs. Minter added her sentiments on the topic while Fiona could barely contain her thoughts. Who were these strangers to comment on Ma? They didn't know her. They'd never listened to her Irish tales or hung on every word of a prayer spoken in her soft brogue.

Da offered Fiona a broad smile that fooled only the lunch guests. Fiona knew better than to miss the warning foretold by his drawn brows and direct stare. "Perhaps after lunch you might show Mrs. Minter the needlepoint you've recently completed."

At the thought of the torture known in polite circles as needlework, Fiona suppressed a groan. Little did Da know that the work she'd done with needle and thread had been to pass the evenings with an excuse not to talk about Da's favorite subject: Fiona's status as a single woman over the age of eighteen.

Pretending to be absorbed in her work had kept Fiona from suffering the embarrassment of discussing which poor fellow Da might feature as a prospective husband. It seemed that since Ma's death two winters ago, Da was more worried than ever about marrying off Fiona and less concerned about allowing her to get the education she must have in order to become a doctor.

Now that the boys had found wives and Da had Douglas, he was beside himself with joy. With each passing year, Fiona knew her brothers' wives would add to the number of grandchildren in the Rafferty family until there would be no end to the Goose Chase, Alaska, branch of the family tree.

While she loved babies and pretty houses as much as the next woman, Fiona believed the Lord had put quite another goal before her. The gift of healing had been entrusted to her, and to ignore that gift seemed to border on blasphemy.

That would be worse than giving up coffee—or fishing.

For that reason, she'd prayed extra hard for just the right opportunity to tell Da of her impending departure. The fact that they had lunch guests must mean the Lord didn't intend her to speak to Da on the issue until dinner.

No matter. She'd been called by the Lord to heal, and nothing would stop her from reaching that goal.

Besides, she'd promised Ma she would follow her dreams wherever they led. And this dream seemed to be leading to a career in medicine.

"Did you hear what the reverend said, Fiona?"

Fiona shifted her attention to the preacher. "I'm sorry, Rev. Minter. What did you say?"

The reverend shook his head. "Understandable. After all, I'm certain if I were about to embark on an adventure of such magnitude, I might be a bit preoccupied, too." He set his fork down and nudged his wife. "Why, I *am*, aren't I?" he said before dissolving into laughter. "I appreciate you allowing us the use of your spare room until the final leg of our journey is upon us."

Da's expression turned somber. "Perhaps we should discuss this after the meal."

Both men looked toward Fiona before concentrating on their plates. Only Mrs. Minter continued to stare.

Fiona cleared her throat and took a bite of corn bread. Still, the woman's gaze bore down on her. "So, Mrs. Minter," Fiona finally said, "what is it that you do, exactly?"

"Do?" The mouse of a woman looked perplexed. "Whatever do you mean, Miss Rafferty?"

Fiona dabbed at the corners of her mouth, then settled her napkin back into her lap. "What I mean is, what sort of talents do you have? What is it you do all day?"

Pink flared on the woman's cheeks, and she cleared her throat. The reverend had stopped chewing to watch the exchange with what looked like interest. Da, however, seemed ready to spring from the chair at any moment.

"Well, I. . ." Mrs. Minter cast a sideways glance at her husband. "During the day, that is, once the reverend is out and about, I. . ." She dropped her gaze to her plate. "I don't suppose I do anything much at all, actually. We'd hoped for children to occupy my hours, but the Lord seems to have had other plans."

The reverend set his fork down and patted his wife's shoulder. "We must thank Him that He's given us a new ministry instead, dear."

Mrs. Minter's smile didn't quite reach her eyes when she said, "Yes, you're right. He has given us that, hasn't He?" A weak hiccup followed the statement, and the pastor's wife began to dab at her eyes.

"Fiona. Apologize at once."

She didn't have to look at Da to know she'd committed a grievous error in judgment. Before she could speak, her father addressed Mrs. Minter.

"You must forgive my daughter. She has delusions of a career." He paused for effect. "In medicine, no less. Can you feature it, Reverend? A medical school wanting to train a girl?"

That did it. Fiona had happily stepped into Ma's role of running the Rafferty home, and she'd even endured the endless hours it took to tie just the right knot and choose just the right colors to make useless needlepoint pillows. To be rewarded by having her choice of career mocked was just too much.

Fiona rose and arranged her napkin on the back of the chair just like Ma used to do. When she cleared her throat and met her father's astonished stare, the room tunneled and contracted until there were only two people present: her and Da.

Shoulders squared, she opened her mouth and let the pent-up words loose. "Perhaps you've missed this fact, Da, but medical schools have been training women for quite some time."

Da's eyes flashed a warning, but he kept a calm expression. "Perhaps you've missed the fact, daughter, that in this family our women are made for a much higher purpose, that of a pursuit in the domestic arts." He looked to the reverend for confirmation. "Have you heard anything so ridiculous as a Christian woman seeking a career?"

While the pastor and his wife shared a quiet chuckle, Da looked completely unamused. Fiona's heart pounded. Slowly, she stepped away from the table, intent on walking away without comment.

Then she spied the look on Mrs. Minter's face. Pity had been replaced by something akin to satisfaction. Fiona's pulse quickened.

"She's been set on this since she was a wee girl. Can you feature it?" Da joined in the laughter.

That, for Fiona, proved to be the last straw.

"I assure you the admissions board at the medical college did not find the issue of my medical training so funny."

She reached into her pocket and withdrew the envelope, depositing it in the middle of Da's plate. He looked down at the paper and knocked the corn bread crumbs off it with his fork. Fiona's breath caught in her throat as her father's gaze scanned the return address.

While Fiona watched in horror, her father tore the letter in half and let it drop to the floor.

"Unlike Mrs. Minter, you have no husband to hold you here, Fiona." The pastor and his wife could not have missed the tremble of anger. "You'll be of much help to Ian and Merry and to Amy and Braden."

Da turned to the Minters and began an explanation of how both his sons were living in the "vast Northland," as he put it. Fiona had heard her father brag of his sons' adventurous streaks and the fine matches they'd made so many times she could practically recite the words right along with Da. This time, however, she could barely hear his voice for the ringing in her ears.

Her father cast a brief glance in Fiona's direction. "The domestic arts are the only career a woman of good character should pursue, don't you think, Rev. Minter?"

"Oh, I do indeed." He turned to his mouse of a wife. "What say you on this, dear?"

Their gazes met. A brief flicker of what may have been sympathy from Mrs. Minter was quickly replaced by a broad smile. "I say that with all those stampeders looking for wives, even a woman not given to cooking and cleaning could do quite well for herself." She punctuated the statement with a smile.

Fiona looked to Da in appeal. Before she could open her mouth, her heart sank. Her father actually looked. . .relieved.

"I had prayed for a solution. After all, she refuses the hand of every suitor who crosses the threshold," he said. "And I feel this permanent arrangement will be beneficial to Fiona."

Well, at least Da thought it a permanent arrangement. Fiona, on the other hand, knew better. The Lord hadn't given her brains so that she might learn to mend a better set of trousers or make a tastier beef stew. And as for those suitors? Contrary to what Da thought, she'd given each one prayerful consideration, then praised the Lord loudly when He deemed them all unsuitable.

She took a breath and let it out slowly. Despite what Da thought, the Lord had made her smart for two reasons: to become a doctor and to figure out how to get out of Alaska. Both objectives, she knew, would take time.

The latter, however, would come soon. All Fiona had to do was keep her outspokenness in check and learn a bit of patience. Surely she could appease her brothers and their wives by fitting into the absurd culture of frozen winters and of summers with no darkness—until she found an escape.

When Fiona dared to look toward the reverend's wife again, she found only pity on the woman's face. But then, Mrs. Minter had no idea Fiona had another envelope upstairs in her room—one that just might save her from a life in the "vast Northland," a life spent in Goose Chase, Alaska.

Taking notice of Fiona's gaze, Mrs. Minter formed her plain features into some semblance of a smile. "Don't worry, Mr. Rafferty," she said sweetly, never removing her attention from Fiona. "We will take good care of your daughter. Have you given any thought to the issue of her transportation? We have acquaintances in Skagway who might be of assistance in seeing that she reaches her destination safely."

As Da warmed to the topic, Fiona returned to her seat and stabbed her knife into the butter, slathering it between layers of corn bread. How she arrived in Alaska was of little concern to her, certainly not worthy of missing a good meal.

Her exit, now, that would be much more interesting.

two

Tucker Smith straightened his back and eased his pick down beside him. A roll of his shoulders loosened muscles hardened from nearly three years of work in this very tunnel.

It didn't start as a tunnel, of course. Way back then, it was just a good idea—a hunch that he and Ian Rafferty had to better themselves and their families by finding gold in the frozen Alaskan land. Who would have known that the discovery of gold in the soil they were digging up for a garden would eventually lead to carving out a tunnel in the face of the mountain?

He cast a glance at the sunlight a few feet away, then turned his back on the day to stare at a wall of midnight-colored earth. Yesterday, he had stood in this same spot, and tomorrow he would do it again.

"Hard to believe I used to complain about working all those hours in the sun back in Texas."

Texas.

The reminder of his home, or rather his former home, made him reach for the pick and begin swinging again. Before long, he'd cut a sizable chunk of rock from the wall. Rubble lay around his boots, and specks of dirt littered the shirt his sister had sewn for him last winter. As he brushed the soft wool, Alaskan earth fell like brown snow.

A glint caught Tucker's attention, and he knelt to nudge the mud away. Pocketing the nugget in the pouch at his waist, he went back to work. By the time Tucker heard Ian coming up the path, he'd made a tidy haul.

"Hey, take a look at this. I think we've found a—" The look on his brother-in-law's face stopped him cold. "What's wrong? Has something happened to Merry?"

"Merry?" Ian shook his head. "It's Douglas, actually."

"Douglas?" Tucker let his pick fall. "What's wrong with the baby?"

"You wouldn't believe it."

Tucker's heart thudded in his chest. If anything happened to his nephew. . .well, he just couldn't imagine what he'd do.

"Rest easy, Tucker. My son rolled over today. One minute, he was on the blanket just as peaceful as can be, and the next, he just flipped right over. Smiled after he did it, too."

Another less jubilant feeling quickly replaced the relief that flooded Tucker. Envy. If not for the way he had turned tail and run from Texas, he, too, might be a papa with a little one he could be proud of.

Tucker took a step back and scrubbed his face with his palms. Where had that come from? Three years had passed since he left home. He knew he still had to work on eliminating the shame he felt over that retreat, but until now, he thought he'd done pretty well handling the rest of it.

Ian gripped his shoulder. "You all right?"

Tucker nodded and reached for his pick. "Yeah," he said as he forced his thoughts back to Ian. "Just happy for you and Merry, that's all."

But as he said the words, Tucker followed up with a silent prayer for the Lord to forgive him for his lack of complete honesty. Sure he was happy, but in equal measure, he compared the blessings the Lord had bestowed on them to the same places where God seemed to have forgotten him.

He probably ought to say something. Ian surely would understand. But then, what good could come of admitting to Ian and Meredith—and to Braden and Amy, for that matter—that he envied the life they led?

No, he didn't need anyone to feel sorry for him. The Lord had blessed him with food in his belly and a warm fire in his cabin at night, even if he did sleep alone. That combined with the presence of Meredith and her in-laws left him hard-pressed to complain.

Still. . .

Tucker swung the pick, felt the satisfying *thud* of metal against rock, and knew he'd have to hit a whole lot of rocks before he came close to forgetting.

If he ever did.

"Oh, I almost forgot." Ian reached into his jacket and retrieved what looked like a letter. "From Seattle. I figured it might be important."

The only person he knew in Seattle was Uncle Darian. The address on the front did not belong to his uncle. "That's odd," he said, as he unfolded the letter and began to read.

"Something wrong?"

"There is, actually. It's Uncle Darian." He looked up at Ian. "He died."

"I'm sorry." Ian rested his hands on the handle of his pick. "What happened?"

Tucker folded the letter and stuck it in his coat. "The letter said he'd been ill awhile but wouldn't let anyone write us. Said he didn't want to bother us with his troubles." He shook his head. "That's Uncle Darian for you. Always worrying about everyone else."

"Yes, that fits with how Merry described him." Ian shrugged. "We'd always hoped to show off Douglas to him someday. I wanted to meet him and shake his hand."

"He would have liked that very much." Another thought occurred to Tucker. "Merry will be upset. There was a time when I tried to convince her to move in with him. Times were hard that first year, and I figured Alaska was no place for a lady, you know?"

Ian nodded. "And while Merry would've been wonderful for him, I have to be selfish and say that I'm glad she didn't listen to you. If she'd been there, we wouldn't be together and we wouldn't have Douglas. Did you think about that?"

When Tucker shook his head, Ian continued. "No sense telling Merry now, since there's nothing she can do about it but fret. Best wait until tonight, and I can tell her."

"No," Tucker said. "You're partly right. We'll wait to tell her, but we're going to tell her together."

Ian studied him a minute. "I reckon that's fair enough."

"Reckon so."

Tucker resumed working, as did Ian. He prayed while he worked; then as generally happened, his prayer turned to humming.

Not too long after, the humming became a full-fledged version of "Rock of Ages." His singing voice resounded in the acoustics of the tunnel.

Awhile later, Tucker laid aside his singing. "I'm going to have to go take care of his affairs. That letter was from a lawyer. Said Merry and I've got an inheritance of some sort."

"You'll have to take care of that before winter."

"And Merry can't go." Tucker shrugged. "Not with the baby so small."

Ian landed a blow on the rocks, then reached for what looked like a decent-sized nugget. "Then it's settled. You'll head for Seattle next week to take care of your business. Tonight, we can talk about how you'll get there and when you'll go."

"I'll need to speak to Merry, but since you're her husband, you ought to know this, too." Tucker met Ian's gaze with a direct stare. "I'm sure Merry told you that our pa left some debts back in Texas." When Ian nodded, Tucker continued. "Well then, I intend to use whatever Uncle Darian left me to settle those. I know we agreed to share anything between us, but I've got to do this. I wouldn't dream of taking anything off

Merry's side, so don't you worry about that."

"I wasn't." Ian laid down his pick. "But he was Merry's father, too, so we'll be shouldering our share. End of discussion."

"No, it's not." In all the time he'd worked and lived side by side with him, Tucker had never wanted to challenge Ian Rafferty to fisticuffs. He was about to change that record when Ian spoke.

"What am I missing here, Tucker? Merry will want to pay for half, and you know it."

"Yes, I know it." Tucker studied the toe of his shoe a moment before lifting his gaze to meet Ian's stare. "I'm telling you that, as the last male in the Smith line, this is my responsibility. I reckon the job of making her understand is going to be your responsibility."

Ian chuckled. "Want to trade with me?"

Tucker went back to his work with a grin. "Not on your life, pal. You chose her for a wife; now you're going to have to live with that."

"That may be," Ian said, "but one of these days you're going to find a wife, and then we'll see."

&

Skagway, Alaska

Fiona began to plot her return to civilization before the ship left the dock in Seattle. The Minters had stayed a full week while Da went about preparing for his only daughter to be shipped north against her will. Keeping mostly to herself, Fiona left her room only to prepare meals.

When the ship left Seattle, she calmly waited in her stateroom until the vessel had cleared the sound. She'd said her good-byes to Da at the farm, knowing the situation was temporary, but even then she'd cried.

By the time they disembarked at Skagway, Fiona had substituted praying for plotting. She'd crafted two more letters, which she mailed early on the third morning in the city.

The reverend and his wife made her feel welcome in their new parsonage, but she itched to get on with the process of settling in Alaska. The sooner she was settled, the sooner she could make her departure. Bad weather and the lack of a suitable guide kept her from taking the land route to Goose Chase.

While waiting for the weather to clear and the ships to begin plying their routes, she settled into an uneasy peace with the Reverend Minter but never managed the same with his wife. Finally the day came when Mrs. Minter gave her the good news: A suitable mode of transport to Goose Chase by water had been secured. She would leave on the morrow.

"How do you feel about fishing?" Mrs. Minter asked.

"Outside of the good Lord and a hot cup of black coffee, that's about my favorite thing. Why?"

A knowing smile had been the only response. Until Fiona set eyes on her mode of transportation, she'd had no idea what that smile meant.

Upon arriving at the docks, however, Fiona realized she'd been booked on a trawler that reeked of the fish it sought. The reverend escorted her aboard and saw her settled into a storage room that was the closest thing to a stateroom before muttering a brief prayer and making a swift exit.

Much as she loved to fish, she generally declined to inhabit spaces within reach of their scent. This time, she obviously did not have that option.

The trip upriver was uneventful, yet Fiona found sleep elusive at night and an object of desire during the day. Finally, when their destination was within sight, Fiona wandered up to the deck.

"I will never get the stench out of my trunk," she muttered as she watched the crew prepare for docking in Goose Chase.

"Oh, I don't know, miss. I find a decent bath and a scrubbing will reduce the smell a bit."

Fiona whirled around to see the elderly captain, a man she now knew to be Mrs. Minter's uncle, Boris Svenson, also known as Captain Sven, grinning in her direction. She adjusted her traveling hat and clamped her mouth shut. No good could come from making a response.

"It helps if ye rinse the first time in saltwater." He shrugged as he stepped over uneven boards with nimble feet, then called out instructions to the crew before turning his attention back to Fiona. "Worked for my wife. She never once complained after I'd scrubbed meself proper," he said as he removed his cap and studied the deck, "may the Lord rest her soul."

"Oh," she said softly. "I'm terribly sorry about your wife."

"Worry not, miss." His downcast look was replaced by a twinkle in his eyes. "The dear woman only wished for my happiness. I've been lookin' for a gal t'keep me warm come winter." He inched closer. "So, you're quite the lovely lass. Are ye meetin' someone special in Goose Chase? If ye are, my niece didn't mention it."

Fiona bit back the caustic words that threatened and forced a smile. "Why, yes, I am," she practically purred. "Two of them, actually."

"Two?"

"Yes, indeed." The smile broadened as she cast a glance toward the little town. "Brothers, actually."

"Brothers?" The captain's busy brows went skyward as he sputtered for a response.

Taking pity on the poor man, Fiona gathered her coat about her. "My, but it's chilly out."

"Chilly? Why, this is practically a heat wave compared to what it's usually like up here. The Lord's been kind in giving us mild temperatures. Just wait until the winter sets in."

Winter? A time when ship traffic ground to a halt due to storms and ice? Oh, no. She'd be long gone before the snow fell.

"Say, would you happen to know when there's another vessel headed back to Seattle?"

"Seattle?" He gave her a questioning look. "Ye haven't even set foot on the shore, and you're already plotting t'leave? I call that downright odd. What say you, Mr. Smith?"

Fiona followed the captain's gaze to a man standing nearby on the shore. Trying to focus through the sun's glare, she made out the silhouette of a shock of dark hair, a pair of broad shoulders, and long legs.

"Well, now. That depends. You didn't propose marriage again, did you, Cap? That's usually why the girls run off." The lanky fellow shifted positions, deepening the shadows covering his face.

An acid reply refused to be restrained. "I'm no girl, sir," she said through clenched jaw. "I'll have you know I'm going to be a doctor."

"A doctor?" The man's voice was deep and decidedly Southern. "I don't believe I've ever met a lady doctor, especially not one wearing such a hat. What sort of odd bird had to be robbed of that feather?"

"And you'll not be meeting this one either, sir." With that, she added a decidedly unladylike frown and turned on her heels. "If you'll excuse me, I believe I've left my other glove in the stateroom."

"Stateroom?" the fellow on the docks called. "Since when does this old tub have staterooms? Cap, did you redo the place when you heard you'd be transporting lady doctors? I sure hope you polish the chandeliers before I board. You know I like things just so."

The sound of the men's laughter sent Fiona skittering below deck. The glove retrieved, she returned to the deck to find both the captain and the arrogant rapscallion gone.

Fiona picked her way across the deck and negotiated the narrow plank that served as an exit, all the while waiting for the irritating man to return so she could educate him on the proper treatment of a lady. Her foot slipped on a patch of ice, and she nearly went sliding toward the dock. Skidding to a stop atop her trunk, Fiona gathered her skirts and her wits.

"It's only temporary," she whispered. "Keep smiling." Then she spied her brothers and the smile broadened.

Braden saw her first and called her name, but Ian outran him to lift her into the air, then envelop her in a bear hug. "Welcome to Goose Chase, Fiona."

three

"Oh! Ian! Put—me—down!" Fiona gave her brother a playful swat as her traveling hat tilted and obscured her vision.

Ian complied, but not before he made one last spin. He set her down on the uneven boards, then feigned exhaustion while Braden grasped her shoulders to keep her from landing on her posterior.

"I didn't expect to see both of you," she said, as she recovered her balance and straightened her hat.

"Amy's visiting her father for a few days." Braden's buttons nearly burst as he straightened his shoulders. "It seems as though I'm going to be a father."

Fiona's squeal of delight nearly drowned out Ian's peal of laughter. While Ian clamped his hand on his brother's shoulder, Fiona wrapped her arms around his middle to give him a tight hug.

"Thank you both," Braden said. "Amy couldn't wait to tell her da."

Ian took a step back. "You don't seem excited about this. What's wrong?"

Braden shook his head. "It's nothing, really. I mean, I know women have babies every day, but. . ."

Fiona reached for her brother's hand and met his gaze with an unwavering stare. "Braden, you can either spend every minute of Amy's time waiting for something to go wrong, or you can open your eyes every day and thank the Lord that He has entrusted you with a new life." She paused to let her statement sink in. "Which will it be?"

"You've grown up, Fifi." Braden swiped at his eyes with

the backs of his hands, then gave her a wry smile. "What happened to the little girl I left behind?"

Ian released his grip on Fiona and reached for her bag. "Braden, you know how she hates to be called Fifi."

The serious moment passed, and her brothers returned to being, well, her brothers. Some things never changed.

Braden chuckled. "I know," he said as he sized up the stack of items she brought. "You still like coffee as much as you did before?"

Fiona gave him a serious look. "More."

"I sure hope you brought some," Ian said. "Tucker's about to drive us mad, worrying you might forget."

"Who's Tucker?"

"That's Merry's twin brother," Ian said. "Remember, I wrote to you about him."

"Ah, yes," she said. "I remember."

"He obviously doesn't know our Fiona." Braden shouldered the bag, grabbed another, then turned to head down the dock. "She wouldn't think of starting a day without a cup, eh, sis?"

"Hey, Braden, remember the time she walked all the way to town for coffee beans because Da wouldn't let her take the horse and buggy out alone?"

"We were out," she said.

While her brothers chuckled and made short work of moving her things, Fiona studied her surroundings. On first glance, Goose Chase seemed nothing more than a collection of ramshackle huts perched alongside a river so narrow it barely supported a decent vessel. In truth, other than the trawler she arrived in, the favored conveyance seemed to be small canoelike rowboats made of what looked to be some sort of hide.

"Am I going to have to ride in one of those?"

"Actually your things are," Ian said. "Most of the time you'll be walking."

She crossed her arms over her chest and stared up at Ian in disbelief. "Walking?"

"Yes, but only if you want to get to your new home," Ian responded.

She bit back the bitter response that would let her brothers know exactly how temporary this situation was. "I'm sorry. That was rude of me." She gave each of her brothers another hug. "I'm afraid the trip's made me unconscionably cranky."

"I don't mind a cranky sister. I'm just glad you're here. I've missed you," Braden said, then added a greeting in his wife's native Tlingit. "That's from Amy. She's thrilled to have you living so near us."

"And Merry can't wait to talk your ear off, I'm sure." Ian shrugged. "I'm afraid our wives are starved for female companionship. I promised to fetch you home as soon as our business in town was done."

"And the baby," Fiona said, "how is he?"

"Douglas is, no doubt, the most brilliant of all the Rafferty men. It won't be long until he's calling me Da."

"Ian, he's only four months old." Braden looked past Fiona to frown. "We're going to have to keep a close watch on Fiona. Look at the attention she's drawing."

Ian followed Braden's gaze. "You're right," he said. "But then, when's the last time an unattached beauty arrived in town?"

"Hush now," Fiona said. "The men can't be that interested in me. I'm as plain as they come. Now let's make haste for home. I've got a nephew and two sisters-in-law to meet."

One glance at the streets of tiny Goose Chase, and Fiona had no doubt her brother's statement *was* true. As she followed them down streets muddy with the beginnings of the spring thaw, she saw men everywhere. Old, young, and every age in between.

And obviously, they all saw her.

"You're causing quite a sensation," Braden said as he steered her away from a particularly large mud puddle. "Like as not there will be a line of suitors at Ian's place before dark."

Ian must have noticed her expression, for he reached to grasp her hand. "Braden, you go on to the mercantile. Fiona and I will wait for you in the *umiak*. I think all this attention's a bit much for her."

Fiona shot Ian a look of thanks, then followed him back to the docks in silence. Somehow her trunk had been transferred to one of the leather-clad canoes. She glanced over at the trawler, then returned the captain's wave.

"Remember the red canoe Da built for us when we were children?" Ian gestured to the leather boat. "This is much like it. It's called an umiak," he explained. "Braden and Amy built it with skins I trapped." He paused. "And we won't be traveling with it all that far." Ian's grin turned tender. "I know all of this is new to you, but I promise you'll love living in Alaska. Just give it a chance."

Once again, Fiona chose not to comment.

As promised, Braden returned quickly, and their trip upriver began. Fiona marveled at her brothers' ability to maneuver the small vessel, given that they used ropes to achieve the task. Many long hours later, they crossed a small bridge and steered the umiak to a stop near a collection of buildings that Fiona prayed were not homes.

Unfortunately, they were.

❧

"Did Da really say that?" Eyes twinkling, Ian Rafferty took a healthy sip of coffee and set the mug on the rough wooden table. His lovely wife, Meredith, swiftly refilled the cup from the pot brewing on the small stove.

A little over two weeks had passed since Fiona had landed in this strange community, and she'd almost caught up with her sleep. While she'd quickly learned to love the women her brothers had married, she had yet to find an equal fondness for the land where they settled. Why, even the bridge that linked her brothers' land to the opposite shore was a temporary structure. Except when they used pulleys and ropes to swing it into position, it stood useless, parallel to the river's edge. Her brothers had explained this was necessary to keep the bridge from causing the water—and the flecks of gold it might carry—to flow away from the opposite shore and the miner who held legal claim to it.

As her brothers had predicted, a constant barrage of suitors seemed to appear at random from the vast wilderness surrounding them. Ian and Braden took great delight in her discomfort, while Meredith and Amy encouraged her to ignore the whole lot of them. Fiona kept her thoughts to herself and counted the days until she could make good her escape.

That morning over breakfast, the talk had once again turned to matchmaking. Unlike before, Fiona spoke up when Ian began his teasing.

"I fail to see what's so funny. Did our father mention that my lack of a mate is the main reason he banished me to this place?" Fiona took a healthy sip of coffee, then glanced over at Meredith, who gave her a nod. "Da feels I should be a wife and mother and not a doctor. To paraphrase, Alaska may do what Oregon did not."

"Get you married off?" Ian shook his head. "And why not? If you haven't noticed, the population in Goose Chase is decidedly male. Why, I'm surprised Merry gave me the time of day, what with the pickings being so plentiful."

Meredith brushed past Ian, pausing only to kiss the top of his head. Fiona watched her disappear behind the fur curtain separating the eating area from the other parts of the tidy-but-claustrophobic abode. While Fiona understood the need to protect its inhabitants from the dreaded Alaska winter, the odd dwelling seemed more like a tomb than a home.

And the facilities, well, to say the least, Fiona did not relish her morning ablutions or the occasional nighttime trip outside. Then there was the complete lack of a proper day and night. She rose and slept by the clock, not the sun, having been warned by Braden on her first day that one might lose track of days and nights unless a diary was kept. Amy advised her that by the time summer set in, she would be able to read a book at midnight.

How her brothers and their families stood it all was beyond Fiona. Even baby Douglas seemed to adapt better than she to the odd life his parents lived.

Fiona forced her mind back to the topic at hand. The courage to speak might not return; seeing the conversation through to the end was best done only once. She took another sip of coffee and stared at Ian.

She would have to have this conversation again with Braden when the opportunity presented itself. Perhaps it was better to divide and conquer when it came to the Rafferty men.

"What if I don't want to be married off, Ian? What if I want to be single the rest of my life so I can devote myself to the calling the Lord's placed on me?"

Shock registered on Ian's face, even as heavy footfalls sounded outside.

A gust of icy wind preceded a tall man bundled into a parka that showed only a pair of brown eyes and a lock of ebony-colored hair. "How did I get so fortunate as to meet the one woman on earth who isn't looking for a husband?" As he peeled off the topmost layer of outerwear, the stranger thrust a gloved hand in her direction. "Tucker Smith," he said. "And you must be Ian's sister, Fiona."

His hand enveloped hers, the fingers strong and warmer than she expected. So was his expression when he removed his cap and shook free a mane of hair that needed a good barbering.

Odd, but something seemed quite familiar about the man.

And the voice? Fiona was almost certain she'd heard that voice somewhere before.

Ian motioned for the man to take a spot at the table, then reached for the coffeepot and a spare mug. "Fiona, meet Merry's brother. Tucker, this is Fiona. He's a Texan, so don't pay attention to half of what he says and ignore the rest of it."

So this was the mysterious Tucker Smith, the man she had heard Meredith and Ian whispering about when they thought she was not listening. Something about a mission to Seattle. A deceased relative whose will needed tending to, perhaps. She'd not been able to piece out the story from her limited knowledge, but truthfully she'd been too tired to muster more than a passing interest.

Fiona sized up Meredith's brother, being careful not to attract his attention. To her surprise, the man acted not at all like the other men who sought her favor.

If Fiona had not been so relieved, she might have been offended.

Tucker shared a laugh with Ian before turning his attention to Fiona. His gaze swept over her, then settled on her eyes. Was that amusement? Recognition?

Surely not.

Ian had written of his brother-in-law and most likely had also told Mr. Smith about Fiona. *Yes, that's why he's staring at me as if he knows me.*

"Well, now, pleased to meet you, ma'am," Mr. Smith said.

The man spoke in a slow drawl, a voice that shook the timbers of her heart with its depth and richness. She wouldn't be surprised to find Tucker Smith had a talent for music, such was the melody of his speech. So this was the mysterious fellow her sister-in-law so often remembered in her prayers.

Tucker settled onto the chair beside Fiona, then swiveled to face her. Rather than stare into the man's startling, sky blue eyes, she settled her gaze on his red suspenders.

Ian leaned forward and rested his elbows on the table. "You get everything handled?"

His yes came out in a weary sigh.

"Were you able to wire the money to Texas?" Merry asked as she pushed back the fur curtain and returned to the room. "I know that was first on your list of things to do after you signed the papers."

"Enough of that." Ian gave Meredith a look of gentle warning. "Let the man rest, dear. He'll give us the details soon enough."

She turned to Fiona. "Tucker's been taking care of some family business. He's been in Seattle for a spell."

Fiona lifted her gaze from the red suspenders to their owner's face. A tinge of the same scarlet color decorated his cheeks. Tucker caught her staring, and she looked away quickly.

Meredith paused beside her husband, but her gaze landed squarely on Tucker. "Funny how the supplies last twice as long when you're away. I think you only came back for the food."

"And I always appreciate the pleasure of your company and the taste of your stew, Merry, so it's no mystery why I'm here." Tucker smiled, and Fiona's stomach did a flip-flop. "The mystery is why you're here, Fiona. What brings a pretty girl to Goose Chase, Alaska?"

When Fiona didn't respond, Tucker looked around the room as if asking for the answer. Thankfully, neither Ian nor Meredith spoke for a full minute.

Tucker gave Fiona a sideways look. "Well, now, a woman with secrets. I'm intrigued."

"Never mind, Tucker," Meredith finally said. "Now tell me all about Seattle."

Fiona sighed. This was a temporary reprieve at best.

Soon, everyone in town would learn why she was banished to this frozen wasteland, and she'd be humiliated for sure. With the ratio of single men to unclaimed women quite out of balance, she'd soon feel the stares, anyway.

Well, no matter, she'd be gone soon enough.

Tucker leaned conspiratorially in Fiona's direction. "Let's make a pact. You keep your secrets, and I'll keep mine. Together, we'll keep this pair guessing. What say you?" Before she could respond, a look passed over his face. "Is. . .that. . . *fresh* coffee?"

Fiona glanced down at her cup, then back at Tucker. "It is. I brought it from home."

"Tucker, you only just returned." Meredith stopped behind her brother to muss his already unruly locks, then smiled at Fiona. "My brother's appetite for coffee is matched only by his appetite for caribou steaks."

"Are we having caribou steaks tonight?" Tucker looked like a kid in a candy store. "Don't tease me, Merry. Seattle is great, but it's not Alaska."

"And I, for one, am grateful." The words were out before Fiona realized she'd spoken them.

"My sister's been banished to Alaska against her will," Ian said to Tucker.

Fiona cringed as she waited for Tucker's sarcastic comment. It never came. Rather, Tucker seemed sympathetic.

Meredith met her gaze. "Same as my brother and me, actually," Meredith said. "Tucker and I never expected we would leave Texas for Alaska. Sometimes your family makes decisions without thinking of how they will affect you, and there's nothing you can do but live with them."

Ian looked stunned at his wife's statement. Tucker, however, rose and put his hands on his twin sister's shoulders. "Sometimes the Lord lets us slide into sticky situations faster than He lets us climb out of them. What happened back in Texas is better left back in Texas. I reckon I'm not willing to say any more than that on the subject, and I'd be obliged if you'd do the same, Merry."

The baby began to whimper, breaking the silence. Meredith looked as if she might speak, then clamped her lips shut. A quick nod of her head was followed by Meredith turning on her heels to follow the sound of her son's cry.

four

Tucker eyed the pretty redhead a split second longer than proper, then forced his attention on his brother-in-law. Something about her tugged at his thoughts. He never forgot a face, and this face he'd seen before. But how was it possible?

He returned to his chair and tried to think of how he might have seen a woman with such fire and promptly forgotten the experience. It seemed impossible.

"You look like you're pondering something important, Tucker," Ian said.

"Do I?" He decided to move his attention elsewhere. Now was as good a time as any to break his idea to them gently. "Did you hear the Harriman Expedition's heading toward Sitka?"

Ian met his gaze. "I did."

"Wonder what you think of that?"

Ian tipped his chair back and ran his hand over his chin hairs. "I reckon somebody's got to do it. We need the maps, and there's no telling what else they'll find." He nodded. "I say, good for them."

That went well enough. Tucker decided to go ahead and spring the whole plan on them. "What would you think if I signed on for the adventure?"

His brother-in-law set his chair down with a *thud*, then shook his head. "Sign on for the adventure? Are you serious?"

Tucker caught the redhead staring at him. "Dead serious, actually," he said. "I met a fellow on the way back from Seattle, a mapmaker. We got to talking, and it turns out they need folks like me who know their way around the tundra." He

33

paused. "So, Ian, what do you think? Can you do without me for a month or so?"

Ian seemed to be taking the news in and chewing on it. Tucker knew his brother-in-law rarely spoke before cogitating a bit. Most times, he liked that about Ian Rafferty. At the moment, however, he was ready to jump out of his seat and shake an opinion out of him. If Meredith hadn't bustled the baby out of the room to feed him, she probably would have spoken her piece by now. He had little doubt, however, what she would say. Ian, on the other hand, just might like the idea.

"I've heard the expedition's going to bring along an artist," Ian's sister said. "How wonderful to see the flora and fauna of the Arctic Circle."

When Tucker looked her way, green eyes stabbed him with something akin to disgust. He made the mistake of chuckling.

"Do you find my statement amusing, Mr. Smith?"

Tucker grimaced. "Forgive me, Miss Rafferty," he said slowly, "but there are more important things in the world than flora and fauna."

"Such as?" Her eyes glinted a challenge stronger than her tone.

"Such as. . ." Dare he hint at the real reason he wanted to be aboard that ship? Probably not. This one seemed to be devoid of the usual cognitive handicaps associated with being born female. Unfortunately, she'd obviously acquired the feminine art of putting a big-mouthed man in his place, most likely a hazard of growing up alongside Ian and Braden. Unless he said something brilliant soon, she'd most likely do just that.

"Such as," he said with false bravado, "making maps so the railroad can go through and towns can be built. You never know when space is going to run out back home in the States. We need to be ready when they start looking for land in our direction." He looked to Ian for support and found only amusement.

Fiona's *harrumph* let him know exactly what she thought of his answer.

"You have a better idea, do you?" His voice rose. "Perhaps a picture of some tree or fern that will save the world?"

Hands on hips, the redhead pushed away from the table and met his gaze. "Or perhaps some plant with medicinal qualities that will save people." Fiona rose. "If you'll excuse me, I have some things to take care of."

He watched Ian's sister sweep from the room as if she were the Queen of England.

"Since when do you want to get on a ship and leave because some fellow down south's living too close to his neighbor?" Ian asked. "Something else is going on here, Tucker Smith, and I want to know what it is."

"I think I know." Meredith's firm reply startled them both.

Tucker whirled around to see his twin sister standing in the doorway, holding Douglas against her shoulder. A look passed between Meredith and her husband, and after a moment, Ian rose. "It's a fine day for a walk down to the creek. I believe I will go see if I can find a bit of gold with the pan."

"That's a fine idea, Ian," Tucker said. "I'll go with you."

Meredith reached him before he stood and pressed her free hand on his shoulder before handing the baby to him. "You're needed here, Tucker," she said. "If Ian needs any help, he can take his sister."

"Take my sister panning? Are you. . ." Ian looked from Meredith to Tucker, then back at Meredith again. "Fishing with Fiona. Ah, yes, of course. Why didn't I think of that?"

"You did," Meredith said. "Just now."

"See what a man needs a wife for?" Ian smiled, then kissed both his wife and his son. A moment later, he was crossing the yard toward the red-haired spitfire.

"See what a man needs a wife for?" Tucker felt the stab of guilt down to his gut. A wife. A son. Maybe a daughter someday. . .

"Tucker."

His twin's gentle voice drew his attention. He looked up at

her and smiled. "Are you going to lecture or listen?"

She settled into the chair next to him and dabbed at the baby's smiling mouth with her handkerchief. Tucker reached for Douglas and held him close against his chest. One hand on the baby's back, Tucker felt the soft fuzz of his nephew's hair tickling his nose. He was, for a moment, lost in the sweet baby smell.

"You won't enjoy him so much when his dinner's digested."

Tucker adjusted his nephew to the crook of his arm and held him slightly away from his body. Meredith giggled and retrieved her son.

"You men never cease to amaze me. You can gut a fish or skin a caribou, but you go weak at the thought of a baby doing what babies do best." She arranged Douglas in her lap, then lifted her gaze to Tucker. "I do believe I know what's wrong, Tucker, but I wonder if you'll say it before I have to."

He shrugged and rose, then reached for the coffeepot. While pouring the last dregs of his favorite beverage into his mug, Tucker watched Ian and Fiona disappear over the rise in the distance.

Alaska was beautiful, especially this time of year. Only Texas held this kind of sway over him, and as the years flew by, the hold of his native land lessened.

The sound of Meredith cooing to her son drew his attention. He turned and took a deep breath, then hauled himself and his coffee back to the table.

"Save me the time and say it, Merry," he said before taking a sip of the hot, strong brew. "No matter what words I might have to defend myself, I am sure you will have more to add to them."

"That's not fair." Meredith's expression softened. "Or maybe it is." She seemed to be searching his face. "I don't pretend to know why the Lord blessed me with Ian and Douglas here in Alaska when you had to leave all your dreams behind in Texas.

I don't deserve all this happiness." Her eyes welled with tears. "And you don't deserve to be alone."

As he expected, his sister knew him too well. Tucker could deny it, but any statement other than the truth wouldn't be worth the breath he wasted on it. Diversion seemed his only option.

"I'm not alone. Between your family and Braden's, I never have to worry about too much peace and quiet." He paused to take a sip of the cooling coffee. "Especially now that Amy and Braden will be giving you a new niece or nephew. Before long, Goose Chase will be overflowing with Rafferty children."

"But that's just it." Meredith shook her head. "Don't bother to deny it. I've seen how you are with Douglas. Oh, Tucker, you should be having babies of your own."

He faked a laugh in another attempt to sidetrack the discussion. "Now wouldn't that be something to see? Last time I checked, it was the wife's job to have the babies."

She tossed her handkerchief at him and rose to walk the baby the length of the room. "Have you written her since we left?"

"Her?" He feigned ignorance. "Since when do I write letters to anyone?"

Meredith halted her pacing. "Stop it, Tucker. You know who I mean."

"Yes, I do know who you mean, and no, I haven't written her." He took a deep breath and let it out slowly. "I told her before I left that I'd never ask her to be tied to a man whose family couldn't hold their heads up in town."

"So that's why you broke it off with her. Because of our father."

His temples throbbed as he tossed back the last of his coffee and set the mug on the table. "No, Merry, I told Elizabeth's daddy that I released her from the promise to me because the situation had changed. She was standing right there when I told him, and she seemed to be fine with it."

"Seemed to be fine with it or struck dumb with shock?" she asked as she patted the sleeping baby's back. "You know, Tucker, you are stubborn as a mule." Meredith paused to shake her head. "No, that's not right. I don't want to insult the mule."

"You, Merry Rafferty, always were the dramatic one."

From the look on her face, Tucker could tell he'd done it this time. He and his twin rarely shared harsh words. Their closeness generally prevented any conflict, but at times like these, it was that closeness that gave him the knowledge of just what words would hit the mark.

The last time they had argued, it had been over a play toy. He couldn't remember who won that argument, but he never forgot how much he hated seeing his sister cry.

Like now.

"And you, Tucker Smith," she said as the first tear wove a path down her cheek, "were always the dense one. You mope around here wishing you had a wife and baby like Ian, yet you went and messed up the one chance you had. No wonder you want to run off and hide on some expedition to the North Pole."

"They're not going to the North Pole. They're—"

"Who cares what the destination is? The only reason you want to be on that boat is to get away from the consequences of your choice. You could have brought Elizabeth with us as your wife, you know."

"Now why would I want to do that? The woman can't brew a pot of coffee to save her life, and she surely doesn't know which end of a fishing pole goes in the water. Why would I want to burden myself with such a woman?"

She refused to be put off track by humor—that much he knew from looking at her. Tucker tried another tack.

"Maybe she didn't want to go, Merry. Have you thought of that? Maybe she didn't want anything to do with a man whose father had no better morals than to defraud half the county."

"It wasn't half the county, and you know it."

"What I know is that I had no choice in what my father did, but I do have a choice about whether to stay here and listen to you telling me what I ought to do."

Tucker rose and headed for the door. If Meredith wanted to question him further on his love life or anything else, she'd have to follow him.

And he intended to walk fast.

≈

Fiona was so mad she could have walked all the way back to Oregon. Instead, she settled for storming away from a conversation where her brother refused to admit that she belonged in medical school rather than Alaska. Ian held the archaic view that his baby sister should be seeking a husband instead of following a dream.

"You're wrong, Ian," she called over her shoulder as she stormed away. "It's not something I want to do; it's something I have to do. There's a difference."

"Oh, Fiona, be serious."

His teasing laughter chased her along the path by the river, and then it brushed past her to echo against the snow-covered hills up ahead. She counted her steps, picking her way around patches of mud and jutting rocks.

How had a lovely stroll with her brother turned into an argument—something she and her brother never had? Ian didn't intend to be mean, and she knew it. He was just a man and, as such, held to a whole bunch of ideas that didn't fit anymore. To listen to Ian Rafferty, one would never know there was a brand-new century dawning in less than seven months.

Fiona would have loved nothing better than to shout back to Ian, reminding him of that fact, but to do that, she'd have to backtrack and catch him where he could hear her. Instead, she allowed herself to think about where she might be when the clock struck midnight on January 1 of the year 1900. She'd be at the medical college, of course.

"What better time to write a letter of acceptance to the university?"

The question, spoken aloud to no one in particular, brought a smile, and she wore that smile until she reached the open door of her temporary home. Once inside, she stopped short when she saw Meredith bent over a sheet of paper, writing furiously. Her sister-in-law seemed so involved in whatever she was working on that she had no idea Fiona stood watching.

"Merry?"

She jumped, grasping her chest. The pen clattered to the floor, where Fiona quickly retrieved it.

"I'm so sorry." Fiona handed Meredith the pen. "I didn't mean to frighten you."

Meredith folded the letter in thirds, then set it aside. "No, it's fine," she said as she smoothed back her hair. "I was just writing a letter to someone back home."

"Would you have extra writing materials I might use? I think I'd like to do the same thing." She gestured behind her. "I think I'll enjoy the outdoors. It's nice out."

"Of course," Meredith said, her voice still a bit shaky. "There's a lovely spot just over the hill beside the river."

When Fiona arrived at the spot, she found it already occupied, so she turned, intent on retracing her steps. Tucker Smith sat so close to the water that he could reach over and stick his hand in if he wanted to. He gave no notice he saw her, and it was only when he called her name that she realized he was aware of her presence.

"Fiona, wait. You don't have to go."

She stopped. "No, I'll find another place to write."

"Suit yourself," he responded without looking in her direction.

Fiona wandered around until she found a secluded spot a

few hundred yards upstream. Spotting a rock large enough to sit on, she perched atop it and hauled out her writing kit. Writing the letter of acceptance took almost no time. It was the letter to her father that she agonized over.

Despite her father's old-fashioned ways, Fiona loved him with all she had. Unlike her brothers, she'd been her father's shadow. Tagging along beside him, baiting his hook, and cooking his meals had cemented a bond between them that nothing could shake.

She might not like his choice to send her to live with her brothers, but she understood it. A man of his generation would never think of letting a woman choose her career, at least not where her father came from.

As much as she did not want to write him of her plans, Fiona knew she must. So with dread and prayers, she began a letter to her father.

She'd used and discarded three sheets of paper when Tucker Smith strolled into sight around the bend in the river. Fiona frowned. Just when she'd finally decided how to break the news to Da. What did the irritating man want now?

He walked tall and swift, making his way over the rocky ground without so much as a glance toward his feet. Unlike her, Tucker had made peace with this place.

"I surrender." He paused. "And I apologize."

Well now, she hadn't expected that. "For what?" came out before she had time to think.

Even an irritating man can look handsome when he grins, and Tucker did. "I won't tell you what Merry called me, but I will tell you she was right."

"I see." Fiona set aside her writing and studied the ink stains on her fingers as she blew out a long breath. "Tucker. . ." She spoke as slowly as she moved, lifting her head as the words fell softly between them. "I owe you an apology, as well. I shouldn't have spoken to you in the manner I did. It was rude."

He reached for a stone to throw toward the river. It hit the middle of the stream with a *plop*, then disappeared below the rippling surface. "We're a fine pair. How about we start over?"

He rose and bowed low, as if he were greeting the Queen of England. "Name's Tucker Smith of the Texas Smiths. The pleasure's all mine." He took two steps back and affected surprise. "Say, aren't you Ian and Braden Rafferty's sister?"

The slightest smile threatened to escape, so she looked away. My, but this one could be charming when he wanted. The last thing a woman on her way out needed was to find an interest in a man who wasn't going with her.

A movement on the other side of the river caught her attention. From where she sat, she watched a silver-haired man slide from behind a rock to crouch beside a stand of trees. "Tucker," she said slowly, "someone is watching us."

five

Tucker follow Fiona's gaze to the other side of the river. He chuckled when the fellow had the gall to wave.

"Do you know him?"

"I'm afraid so." He returned his attention to Ian's sister. "That's Mr. Abrams. He owns the land on that side nigh on up past the creek."

"Does he always spy on the goings-on over here?"

"Well, I can't be sure." Tucker shrugged. "But I believe he busies himself with working his claim most days. Leastwise, Merry's never complained about him."

She clutched her paper and ink. "Wonderful."

"Looks like you've caught his attention. Maybe he can't help staring because he thinks you're the prettiest thing he's seen in some time."

The expression on Fiona's face told him how little she liked that idea. Tucker hoped his own expression didn't give away how much of that statement described his feelings, as well.

"So he's not dangerous?" Fiona swung her gaze in his direction before taking another look at the fellow across the river. "Are you sure? He seems a bit. . .well. . .odd. Look, he's climbing that tree."

"Miss Rafferty," he said slowly, "I assure you, old Mr. Abrams isn't any more dangerous than I am."

She cut him a sideways glance. "And that's supposed to make me feel better?"

For a minute he couldn't tell whether or not she was serious. Then her lip twitched, and he knew she was hiding a smile.

A cry for help prevented Tucker from answering. Fiona

43

jumped to her feet and raced toward the sound.

"It's your neighbor," she called, as she jumped off the rock and searched for a spot to cross the river. "I think he fell out of the tree. Look!"

She pointed to Abrams, who lay on the ground. Tucker stood watching for a moment, until he realized the panicked female was about to try and swim across.

"What are you doing?" Tucker called. "The water's freezing. You can't go in there." He caught up to her. "Go back and fetch Merry. She will know what to do."

"There's no time," she said. "Get me across the river." When he didn't react immediately, she took off walking again.

"Miss Rafferty, what are you doing? If you get in the water, you'll—"

"Help me across, then, or I'm swimming. That man needs medical attention and I have the training." As if to prove her point, she made a move toward the first rock nearest the banks. "I can walk across the rocks and—"

"Not on my watch. Ian would have my hide. The bridge is only a quarter mile downstream."

Fiona shook her head. "No time to go that far. He could be seriously injured. There has to be a faster way."

Making up his mind as he sprinted after her, Tucker swept the obstinate woman into his arms, then swung her over his shoulder. "Be still, or we'll both get a good dunking. I'm crossing up ahead where that fallen log is. If you understand that you need to be completely still, say yes now. Otherwise, I'm dumping you right here."

"Yes" came like a squeak from somewhere behind his right ear.

Tucker hauled her closer against him and tested his balance on the log. Before putting his next foot forward, he paused.

"What are you doing?" the Rafferty woman croaked. "Time's wasting."

"Hush, woman," Tucker said, "I'm praying; then I'm crossing. You got any complaints about that, you take it up with the good Lord."

She held silent and still while he finished his prayer and set across. Midway across the stream, Tucker stopped to readjust the slight weight he carried over his shoulder. To his surprise, she neither moved nor spoke.

Three steps later, however, she squealed and grasped handfuls of his shirt when his foot slipped. Tucker righted himself and made the rest of the trip across in short order. As soon as he set her feet on the ground, Fiona began running.

When she reached the fallen man, she dropped to her knees and began to examine him. A half hour later, she had Mr. Abrams trussed up and ready to transport. While Fiona waited with the patient, Tucker raced back to the cabin. Ian and Meredith were in the middle of an animated discussion.

"It's Abrams," he called as he reached the clearing. "Fiona's got him situated, but he's not waking up. She says he needs to see the doc over in Goose Chase."

As quickly as possible, the men used the pulleys and ropes to swing the bridge out across the river until it came to rest on the opposite bank. Ian followed Tucker back over to where Fiona waited.

"Any luck in reviving him?" Ian asked.

Fiona shook her head. "His pulse is slow but regular, and his pupils are even, but he's completely nonreactive. I'm afraid there might be swelling on the brain that can only be relieved in an operating room."

Neither Tucker nor Ian moved. Other than the nasty bump rising on Mr. Abrams's head, he looked as if he might be taking a nap rather than fighting for his life.

Fiona jumped to her feet. "What are you waiting for? This man could die if we don't get him help!"

Ian spoke first. "Fiona, honey, I don't think you realize what it would take to get him to town. You're not in Oregon anymore. It's a half-day's walk, not a ride on a train or a buggy."

Tucker watched while the redhead's expression changed from worried to determined.

"Then we walk. Which of you will go with me?"

Before he realized what he'd said, Tucker agreed to the trip. Ian slapped him on the back and wished them well, then helped Tucker get Mr. Abrams situated in the umiak. Meredith insisted on packing a meal for the trip.

Fiona, however, was only concerned for her patient. She did, however, agree to take a letter from Meredith to the post office in Goose Chase. After all, she had a pair of letters to mail, too.

Fiona set her bag and Meredith's pail of food into the vessel beside the patient, straightened her traveling hat, then reached for the rope. The sooner they left, the faster they would get there.

"What are you doing?" Tucker gestured to the umiak. "Get in and ride. This is no place for a lady to be walking."

Her jaw set in a determined line, she ignored him and tugged on the boat's line. It barely moved. Tucker let her work at it a moment longer; then he reached past her to take the rope away.

"If you want to get him to town in time, you're going to need to cooperate with me. Which one of us has been here longer?"

She looked up, and for the first time, he noticed the upturned tilt to her nose. He could tell from her expression she didn't like the answer to his question.

"You," she finally said.

"Then would you let me lead?" He took her hand and met her gaze. "Please," he added in deference to her pride.

"If it will get Mr. Abrams to the doctor sooner, I will do as you ask." She slipped her hand from his and stepped into the umiak. Tucker pretended not to notice how the boat rocked as its newest passenger landed unceremoniously on her posterior. There would be plenty of time for teasing once they reached Goose Chase.

In the meantime, he would keep his peace, and hopefully, so would she. If only she knew how badly he wanted to start by asking her just what fit of insanity she'd been in when she purchased that ridiculous hat.

ଈ

Fiona sat stock-still while the vessel slid over the sparkling water. They confronted the crisp wind head-on, and waves lapped up the sides. On occasion, the breeze tried to lift her hat off her head, but the hat pin held it tight and close.

At regular intervals, Fiona dipped her handkerchief in the water and bathed Mr. Abrams's face. Once she thought she saw him blink, but other than that, the older man remained unresponsive.

By the time they reached Goose Chase, Fiona had begun to wonder if the injured man would ever regain consciousness. Tucker pulled the boat ashore and helped Fiona stand.

Her legs complained as Fiona tried to coax them to co-operate. Tucker refused to let her slip from his grasp as they made their way to solid ground. "You wait here, and I'll go fetch Mr. Abrams."

"Wait," she called. "Don't move him yet. How far is the doctor's office from here?"

"Just over there. It's the one with the white porch rail out front," he said, pointing to a wood-frame building several blocks away. "Best I can tell, the only way to get him there is to carry him."

Fiona considered the statement a minute, then nodded slowly. "It's not so far that he'd be injured any further, but, please, be careful."

Tucker went back to the boat and gently lifted the unconscious passenger. Fiona marveled as the miner made carrying the older man look easy.

Racing to keep up with Tucker's long strides, she was nearly out of breath by the time they reached the building with the white porch railing. The sign above the door said R. KILLBONE, PHYSICIAN. Directly beneath that, a hand-lettered note urged prospective patients to knock and come straight in. Bill collectors, the sign went on to state, should knock twice, and then wait for the doctor to answer.

Fiona knocked, then tugged the door open and held it wide until Tucker disappeared inside. She followed the path Tucker took. A neat living area gave way to a room that looked as if it had once served as a bedroom. A worktable stood in the center of the room and a small bed in the corner.

"Doc, you here?" Tucker called.

"That you, Tucker Smith?"

"Yes, sir. I've got a patient for you. It's Mr. Abrams. He fell out of a tree."

A spry man with a shock of dark hair and a pair of wire spectacles came around the corner. "What do we have here?" He noticed Fiona and nodded. "Who're you?"

"She's a Rafferty, Doc. Ian and Braden's sister."

Fiona offered her hand, and he shook it. "Fiona Rafferty, Doctor. Pleased to meet you."

"Likewise, I'm sure." The doctor studied her a moment before turning his attention to Tucker's nosy neighbor. Fiona watched him begin his examination of the older man.

"His pupils are reactive to light," she offered. "There's been no change since this morning."

Doc Killbone looked at Fiona over his spectacles. "You got formal doctor training, miss?"

"No, sir, not yet, but I'm hoping to remedy that soon." She avoided Tucker's gaze. "I did what I could to stabilize the gentleman, but he's not come out of this since he fell. I'm a little concerned about the contusion on his forehead."

"Hmm, yes." The doctor turned his back on Fiona and completed his examination.

While the doctor worked, Fiona snuck a glance over at

Tucker only to find him already staring at her. She looked away quickly, then chastised herself for acting like a schoolgirl.

"Is there anything I can do to help, Dr. Killbone?" she asked.

"You say you know your way around an operating room?" When she nodded, he started barking instructions. Before she knew it, Fiona was assisting the doctor in treating the older man.

"If you two don't need me, I'm going to go see if the things I ordered came in at the mercantile. I'll meet you back here in a while."

"All right by me, Tucker," the doctor said.

Fiona watched Tucker disappear down the hall before turning her attention back to the patient.

At one point, the doctor paused to nod his approval. "You're a natural, miss," he said. "You ought to go ahead with that training as soon as you can. I won't be doctoring around here forever, so I'll need someone to take over my practice."

Rather than explain to him that she'd never return to Alaska once she made good on her escape, Fiona concentrated on the compliments about her doctoring skills that he paid her. When the doctor completed his work, he stepped away to wash his hands in the corner basin. As he toweled dry, he turned to appraise Fiona.

"I don't think I've ever said this to anyone, so you listen close to me, you hear?"

"Yes, sir."

"I've seen a lot of doctoring in my life, but what you did for that man most likely saved his life." He let the towel drop into the basin. "Where are you set to study at?"

Fiona patted the letter in her pocket. "Oregon, sir. I've been accepted into the medical college there."

The doctor rocked back on his heels and studied her again. "That's a fine school, young lady. You ought to do well there. When do you start?"

Emboldened by his praise, she pulled the letter from her

pocket. "If this letter reaches the school in time, I plan to start with the new term."

"I'm going to do something to help that along," the doctor said. "My nephew's headed back to Washington State two days from now. What if I were to have him take the letter as far as Seattle? From there, he can see it gets put in the mail. That way, the letter will reach its destination a whole lot faster and a might safer."

Her heart and her hopes soared. "Would you? That would be. . .wonderful."

The doctor's eyes narrowed. "Now, I'm going to ask a favor of my own." He paused. "I was serious when I said I wanted to know I'd have someone to take over for me if ever I couldn't do my job. You willing to do that, Miss Rafferty?"

Would she? Leaving Alaska for good had always been her plan. Still, what were the odds that the doctor would actually want her to return? And if he did, the Lord would handle the details.

Fiona took a deep breath and let it out slowly. "Oh, yes, sir."

"All right. One more question. Do you have your passage set for Oregon?" When she didn't immediately respond, he gave her a knowing look. "You were going to decide on that when the time came?"

She nodded. "I suppose so."

"You leave that to me. I want you back here one week before the term starts. I'll have your ticket ready." He adjusted his glasses. "And lessen you think I've got designs on you, plan to travel alone."

Fiona released the breath she'd been holding and smiled. "Thank you."

Dr. Killbone shook his head. "You just hold off on those thanks. You may want to wring my neck when I call in this favor and ask you to come up here and take over for me."

six

Tucker walked into the mercantile like a man on a mission. Bypassing the usual departments, he stepped cautiously into the women's section.

"Merry needing something?"

Tucker turned to see the proprietor of Benson's Mercantile heading his way. "Well, not exactly." He filled the older gentleman in on what he wanted.

"You'll be needing to speak with Mrs. Benson," he said. "Oh, and before you leave, don't forget to pick up those things you ordered last time you were here."

A half hour later, Tucker returned from his errand to find Doc and Miss Rafferty still in the room with Mr. Abrams. He excused himself, retraced his steps, and waited outside the doctor's office as long as he could before he started pacing.

While he walked, he let his thoughts churn. The woman in the office right now was not the one he thought he'd met at the Rafferty cabin. This person was cool and confident, a woman at home in a place where medicine was practiced.

The silly sister of Ian and Braden did not exist there. Rather, she looked to be in her perfect environment.

Why, then, was Tucker so disappointed to figure this out? He'd only just met the girl.

The door opened, and the object of his thoughts appeared, closely followed by Doc Killbone.

Tucker stopped his pacing to shake the doctor's hand. "How's my neighbor?"

"The next few hours are crucial. Like as not he'll wake up tomorrow with a nasty headache and a strong regret that he climbed the tree in the first place."

"I'll sit with him tonight so Doc can get some sleep." Fiona reached into her handbag and pulled out three letters, then handed one to the doctor. "I'm going to go mail these; then I'll serve up whatever Merry sent. How's that?"

"I'd say that sounds like a good plan."

She nodded and took two steps away, then turned on her fashionable heels. "You do have coffee, don't you, Doc?" When he nodded, she looked relieved. "Good. I can put up with just about anything. . . ." She looked at Tucker, then back at the doctor. "But I'm not fit to be around if I miss my coffee."

The men shared a chuckle as Fiona resumed her walk across Main Street.

Tucker turned to the doctor. "I'd best get down to the boardinghouse and make my arrangements before Widow Callen runs out of beds."

"No, need, son," the doctor said. "I've got plenty of space upstairs." He gave Tucker a sideways look. "My boy and me will be here to chaperone, and Miss Rafferty will likely not leave the exam room all night, so I don't see anything improper in the arrangement, do you?"

Tucker studied the subject of their conversation a moment. "No, sir," he finally said. "I can't see anything wrong with the arrangement. Besides, Miss Rafferty's practically family."

"Be that as it may, she's still a fine woman," the doctor said after Fiona disappeared into the postal office. "And one of these days, she'll be a fine doctor." He clapped his hand onto Tucker's shoulder. "You got designs on her, Tucker?"

"Designs? On that one?" He tried to look casual. "Do I look crazy?"

"No," the doctor said. "That's why I'm asking."

≈

The next morning, Tucker was still thinking about the doctor's question. Finally, he had an answer. While he did admit she was a pretty little thing, even with the silly hat, and she'd stood up to the challenge of keeping nosy Mr. Abrams alive, she wasn't the type to settle down and have a family.

So, much as he hated it, the answer to the doctor's question was no.

He knew this for sure as he watched Fiona climb into the umiak. He questioned it only for a moment when they stopped to let her climb out and walk a spell. She hadn't asked about the package he had deposited at her feet, which earned her high marks.

Last thing he could abide was a nosy female.

She'd also stayed awake despite the fact that he doubted she'd had much sleep. Much as he hated to slow down their trip home, he probably ought not walk her so fast. When he adjusted his pace, Fiona looked relieved but held her tongue.

They walked along in silence until Fiona spoke in a wistful voice. "Do you ever get used to how beautiful it is here? Look at the mountains over there."

Tucker nearly stumbled when he followed her directive, so for the next hour he ignored her completely. Finally the growling in his stomach could no longer be ignored, so he hauled the umiak onto shore and retrieved the food Doc had insisted on sending.

They ate in silence, more due to Tucker previously ignoring Fiona's chatter than anything else. The girl was smart. It didn't take her long to figure out he wasn't going to be much of a talker on this trip.

The sun felt warm on his shoulders as Tucker eased back against the rock, his stomach full and his eyes heavy. When he opened them again, he was alone.

He didn't panic until he heard the scream. Women often overreacted in his estimation. Like as not, the source of her upset was a harmless bug or some other such thing.

He waited a moment. "Fiona?" he finally called.

No answer. Then came, "Mr. Smith!" in the form of a second scream.

Tucker scrambled to his feet and bolted off the rock. The sound came from the south, the opposite direction from the river. What in the world was Fiona doing heading off in that direction?

"Fiona, are you all right?"

No answer.

She screamed his name a third time. A second of silence followed.

Tucker found her teetering on the edge of a rock just beyond his reach. She seemed, on first glance, to be completely fine.

"Fiona, that's not funny. Come down right now before I come to my senses and get mad."

She neither moved nor spoke. Rather, she edged a bit to the left, then froze. "I—I can't," she finally said.

He moved a few steps closer. "You can't what? Come down? That's ridiculous."

"No," came out more like a squeak than a word. "I'm stuck."

"You're what?"

She tried to look over her shoulder but teetered and lost her balance. Tucker was there in an instant, catching her just in time.

She landed with a *thud* against his chest, and he held tight to her. The only calamity was her hat, which fell into the dirt at his feet. Tucker took a step to balance himself, and unfortunately, one boot landed on the thing.

At least he'd saved Fiona. She could buy another hat.

As he looked down at the woman in his arms, two emotions hit him hard. First, he felt like laughing. Then, much to his surprise, he felt like shaking her for the fright she'd given him. He set her on her feet and moved off the silly hat, then took two steps back.

"Thank you," she said, assuming her regal bearing once more.

Stifling a smile, Tucker asked the obvious question. "Miss Rafferty, how did you come to be standing on that ledge?"

"I thought to reach that secluded spot."

Tucker looked up in the direction where she pointed and saw the stand of trees. "Why did you want to get up there?"

To Tucker's surprise, the redhead's cheeks flamed to match her hair. "That's rather private, and I'd prefer not to say."

Fiona spied her hat and retrieved it, then studied the bent feather. Knocking the dirt off it made the thing wearable, but the feather would never be the same. Still, the contrary woman set the atrocity atop her head and turned on her heels.

"In the future," he said to her retreating back, "you might want to think twice about wandering off. This time the only danger was falling, but there could be any number of hungry wild animals out there."

"I doubt that, Mr. Smith. If such a danger existed, I'm sure a competent guide such as yourself would have warned me before we set off."

She had him there. He decided to try another tack. "Miss Rafferty, I have to ask. Why didn't you just climb down? Was it those prissy shoes you're wearing?"

"Prissy shoes?" Her shoulders shrugged, but she did not slow down. "I'll have you know these shoes were chosen specifically because they are not only serviceable but also quite attractive and fashionable."

"Well, now, they might be all that, but they are also a menace. Still, if you say they didn't keep you from climbing down, I'll have to believe you."

She picked up her pace. The bent feather bobbed faster. "Yes, I suppose you will," she said. "Now can we change the subject?"

"I'm agreeable to that," Tucker said, "except that my original question still hasn't been answered. Why didn't you just climb down instead of hollering your fool head off and then nearly falling to your death?"

"To my death? My, how you do exaggerate, Mr. Smith."

She sounded a bit out of breath, most likely from the speed she'd chosen to walk. It seemed like the madder he made her, the faster she walked. At this rate, they'd be back to the cabin in record time. He watched the crooked feather on her hat bob up and down and gave thanks for that.

Far be it from him to slow her down, so Tucker decided to give her more reason to race ahead. "So, one more time I'll ask. Why didn't you climb down, Miss Rafferty? And this time, no nonsense. Just give me the plain truth. I promise not to laugh."

Fiona stopped abruptly and whirled around. Tucker nearly slammed into her. "You want the plain truth?"

Tucker looked down into eyes that sparked with anger, and all he could think of was how the freckles on her nose matched the color of her hair just right. He'd have kept staring indefinitely if she hadn't stabbed his shoulder with her forefinger.

"The truth is—" She paused to look away. Without warning, she swung her gaze back to collide with his. "Because I didn't know I was afraid of heights until I got up there. Are you happy now?"

He wanted to laugh, but the look on Fiona's face warned him against it. Instead, he decided to keep his mouth shut. He'd learned in his dealings with Meredith that some questions were best left unasked, especially in regard to the peculiarities of women.

"Yes, I suppose I'm happy as can be, considering the circumstances and the company."

Fiona made a sound of disgust and picked up her skirts, heading toward level ground at a fast clip. As he watched her pick her way across the rocky terrain, Tucker thought of the contents of the package in the umiak.

Perhaps now was the time to get her situated in something sensible, something she wouldn't break her neck wearing.

The moment the thought occurred, Tucker saw Fiona's

expensive footwear catch between two stones. She pitched forward and began to stumble, then caught a branch just in time.

With an I-told-you-I-could-take-care-of-myself look, Fiona stared up at him. "I'm fine."

The branch broke. Fiona Rafferty tumbled into the water.

❧

When Fiona hit the water, all the air went out of her lungs. She sputtered and clutched at the icy liquid until she felt something solid.

As her head came above water, she saw the thing she'd grasped on to was the broken tree branch. At the other end of it crouched Tucker Smith.

"This branch is old and nearly dried out, so I'm going to have to be real careful pulling you in with it. If we get to going too fast, it'll break. Do you understand?"

"Yes, I understand." The feather from her hat clung to her face, and she swiped at it, sending the hat flying.

"Don't you dare try and fetch that thing, Miss Rafferty. It's not worth drowning for."

"Under the circumstances," she said as she watched her prized traveling hat float downstream with the current, "perhaps you should call me Fiona."

"Fiona, it is, and I'm Tucker," he said. "Now listen carefully. The longer you're in that water, the less likely you are to think straight. That water's still cold. Now, tell me if you can still hang on while I finish pulling you in."

All she could do was nod and wrap her fingers tighter around the rough bark. She looked toward the umiak sitting on the bank. "What about the boat? Can't you get in it and come after me?"

"To do that, I'd have to let go of the stick. You want me to do that?"

She thought a minute. "I guess not, but do you have a better idea?"

"While I pull, I'd be much obliged if you'd start to praying. The Good Book says the Lord pays particular attention when two or more are praying the same thing." He gave the branch a gentle tug. "Oh, and if you were of a mind to, you might pray I don't fall in after you. Between us, we've only got one set of dry clothes."

Fiona did her best to pray and hold tight to the branch, but the harder she tried at both, the more difficult they became. Finally, she closed her eyes and let the waves lap against her as she rested her chin on the branch. The current swirled, causing Fiona's skirts to tangle around her ankles and making it nearly impossible to kick her legs.

Now her only lifeline was the broken tree limb. Without warning, it snapped.

Fiona's feet slammed against the river bottom, and she jerked to attention. Pushing off, she lunged toward the bank. Tucker hauled her onto dry land. Immediately, her teeth began to chatter.

"Fashionable and attractive indeed," Tucker said as he pulled the offending shoe off her foot and tossed it toward the middle of the stream. A second later, the other shoe suffered a similar fate.

Before Fiona could protest, Tucker hauled her onto her feet and handed her a wrapped package. She wanted to ask what it was, but her mouth refused to form the words.

Tucker turned her away from him and pointed to a stand of trees. "Go on, now, and get dry. You have my word as a gentleman that I won't turn around or open my eyes until you tell me to."

While she watched, he turned his back to her and climbed into the umiak to sit. Fiona clutched the package to her chest and tried to decide what to do. It didn't take long to realize that although it was summertime, wearing wet clothing in Alaska was foolhardy at best.

Fiona slipped deep into the stand of trees and, as quickly as she could, exchanged her dress for a blue wool shirt that dipped past her knees and a pair of denim pants with legs much too long for her. The only item in the package that came close to fitting was a pair of fur-covered boots.

She walked out of the foliage with one hand on the overlarge trousers and the other clutching her dripping clothes. Tucker still sat inside the umiak with his back to her.

"Is that you, Fiona?"

"Don't you say one word, Tucker Smith. Not one."

True to his word, Tucker didn't move, even when Fiona tossed the bundle of wet clothing into the boat. As Fiona came around to face him, she saw his eyes were closed. He did, however, seem to be having difficulty keeping a straight face.

With what little pride she could muster, Fiona stepped into the boat and sat next to Tucker. "Can we go home now?"

"I'll need to open my eyes."

"Not one word." Fiona released a long breath. "And no laughing."

Tucker opened his eyes, then shut them again. When he didn't move, Fiona poked his arm.

"What are you doing?"

He cut her a sideways glance. "Trying to remember if I made a promise about not laughing."

The trip back to the cabin consisted of Fiona riding and Tucker holding the rope. Neither said a word.

When Fiona walked into the cabin, all conversation stopped. Meredith sat beside Amy, who held baby Douglas in her lap. Fiona left her wet clothing on the doorstep and brushed past them to step into the other room.

"Are those new boots?" Meredith asked.

"They're very nice," Amy added. "Aren't they, Douglas?"

The baby grinned and made a cooing sound.

"It's the rest of the outfit I'm a bit confused about." Meredith leaned forward. "Did Tucker help you pick it out, by any chance? I could have warned you the man has no concept of fashion."

Fiona stuck her head out of the door. "Hush, both of you," she said before dissolving into a fit of laughter.

seven

Three days later, when Tucker hadn't come around the cabin, Fiona went to him. She heard him rather than saw him, the sound of the pickax keeping time with a remarkably good version of "Rock of Ages."

She'd tucked the clothes she borrowed under her arm, along with the odd, fur-covered boots. As an added thanks, she'd wrapped one of Meredith's oatmeal cookies and placed it along with Tucker's lunch in the pail.

Rather than interrupt him, Fiona waited until he got to the chorus and began to sing along. Soon the baritone stopped, and she was left to sing soprano alone.

"I brought your clothes back. Oh, and since you've been avoiding Merry's cabin, she sent lunch," she said when he emerged from the tunnel.

She waited for a response and was rewarded with a combination of silence and an irritated glare. Evidently, the man had forgotten his manners somewhere between Goose Chase and the mine.

"And I wanted to thank you for saving my life."

Tucker let the pick drop and massaged the back of his neck. "Which time?"

He wore a blue shirt nearly identical to the one she'd washed, and he'd left it unbuttoned to reveal a pristine undershirt over dirt-covered trousers. A streak of black mud decorated his right cheek, and it was all Fiona could do to keep from walking over and wiping it off with the corner of her apron.

Fiona set the clothing on a tree stump, then situated the boots on top. "Fair enough." She took a step back and studied her ragged nails. "I was wondering something."

Tucker exhaled loud enough to be heard across the distance between them. His stance told her she'd interrupted something important; the facts stated the opposite. After all, it was near to lunchtime, and the gold he hunted sure wasn't going anywhere.

She almost said just that, but she needed his cooperation. "You're leaving to go with the Harriman Expedition, right?"

He leaned against the handle of his pick and shook his head. "You came all the way out here to ask me that? Merry could have answered you and saved you a walk. Besides, I'm not going to take you with me, much fun as that proposes to me."

So his mood hadn't improved.

"I know I'm not your favorite person." At this, Tucker's head jerked up, and he looked as if he wanted to speak. When he said nothing, she continued. "But I don't belong here. I believe the Lord's got other plans for me than to stay here in Alaska and become some stampeder's wife."

When Meredith's brother did not react, she decided to say out loud the thing she'd been holding in her heart since she left Goose Chase. To say anything to Tucker would be dangerous, especially given his mood. If Meredith got wind of her plan, she would tell Ian, and then the jig would be up. Like as not, they'd bundle her off to the far reaches of Alaska before any of them would send her off with their blessings.

Fiona drew in a deep breath of crisp air, then let the words escape. "I've been accepted to medical college. All I need is a way to get to Oregon before the term starts."

Tucker yanked his pick up and slung it over his shoulder. In long strides, he reached the tunnel. "I know," echoed over his shoulder as he disappeared.

"You know?" She stared incredulously at the empty opening of the man-made cave. "You know?"

How dare Tucker dismiss her like that? Didn't he realize the risk she'd taken by welcoming him into her confidence?

Hands on her hips, Fiona called to the obstinate miner. His only response was a rhythmic *ping. . .ping. . .ping* from deep in the tunnel.

So that's how he was going to be. "Well, Mr. Smith," she muttered, "I think you've forgotten I grew up with two brothers. I learned early on that if the bear won't come out of the cave, you go to the bear."

The tunnel was dark and narrow, barely large enough for a man of Tucker's size to stand upright. The smell of dank earth was nearly overpowering. So was the presence of Tucker Smith.

She watched his shoulders bunch and the muscles in his arms flex as he slammed the pick against the rocks. "Tucker Smith, we're going to finish this conversation whether you like it or not."

"No, Fiona, we're not." Tucker didn't spare her a glance as he went back to the task at hand. "And I'm prepared to work until sundown with you standing there pouting. I think you've forgotten I grew up with a sister."

Ping. . .ping. . .ping.

"Is that so?" Fiona willed her anger to abate, clearing her mind for a better use of her thinking skills—outwitting Tucker Smith. "Well," she said slowly, "perhaps you're right."

*Ping. . .ping. . .*pause. "What did you say?"

She didn't dare look at him. Rather, she turned to study the dirt wall. "I said, perhaps you're right." *Time to look him in the eyes.* "I can't fool you. You're too smart for me."

"I hope you don't think you can fool me into making a decision." He inhaled and closed his eyes. "Because it won't work," he said as he exhaled.

"But Tucker, I—"

"Out." His voice was low, even, and held more than a little irritation. Yet that sentiment didn't quite reach his eyes, which were twinkling with what she hoped was amusement. "Whatever you're up to, it won't work. Go home."

"That's just the thing, Tucker. I'm trying to go home." Fiona shuffled her feet in the hard-packed dirt. "Well, to be exact, I'm trying to go to my new home."

He shook his head. "Have you ever considered you might already be home?"

"Not even for a minute."

Tucker pushed a lock of hair out of his eyes. "You don't think maybe God's got a purpose for you right here in Alaska?"

Fiona straightened her shoulders and looked Tucker Smith in the eye. Unfortunately, the snippy answer she wanted to give refused to come out. Instead, words that couldn't possibly have originated with her popped out of a mouth too surprised to stop them.

"As much as there's a need for wives in Alaska, there's a greater need for doctors, don't you think?"

❧

Tucker hated to admit too quickly that the girl had a point, so he pretended to cogitate on her statement. As much trouble as she'd caused him just traveling to and from town, he truly couldn't imagine her taking on the life Meredith and Amy lived.

Before the first year was out, the poor man she married would head for the hills or, more likely, drown in the river trying to fish her out. Still, Tucker knew that if he helped Fiona, he'd have her brothers to answer to.

And worse, he'd most likely have to give an explanation to Meredith.

"Well?" she urged. "Will you help me?"

He thought of Ian and how slow the man was to respond. Maybe that approach would buy him some time. "Let me think about it," he said.

Fiona's smile set his teeth on edge. Worse, she looked like

she might be getting ready to thank him. Considering he hadn't promised to help her, he surely couldn't accept any appreciation.

Then there was the problem of their close proximity. Compared to the dirt around them, she sure smelled nice.

Tucker cleared his throat. "Don't you need to go help my sister?"

"No," she said. "Not until later. She went over to Mr. Abrams's place to help his niece get settled in. It was my job to pull the weeds in the garden, and I finished that already."

"Wait. Abrams has a niece?"

The redhead nodded. "Evidently so. At least she claims to be."

"Really? Did she bring her uncle home?"

"No," Fiona said. "Mr. Abrams won't be well enough to travel for another week. Violet was fortunate to find her way here with that fellow who delivers the mail."

"I see." Tucker turned his back on the woman and said a quick prayer for strength. As much as he liked to look at the pretty girl, he'd much prefer to do so from a distance.

"Merry said you'd like Violet." She paused and seemed to be thinking over something. "She said Violet was an answer to prayer."

"Is that so?" Tucker reached for his pick and hoped he was wrong about his sister's motives for befriending the Abrams woman. "Well, now that you've caught me up on all the news, you can go on to wherever you were headed next."

"I told you I've got nowhere else to be right now. Besides, that's not all." She leaned toward him. "I felt I should warn you."

"About what?"

"About Violet Abrams." She paused. "And your sister." She shook her head. "You probably aren't interested. Although. . ."

Tucker hated to ask, yet he couldn't help himself. "Although what?"

Fiona shrugged. "Although I felt like a man would want to know when he was about to be set upon by a pretty girl. She's looking for a husband, you know."

He studied the intruder. "She shouldn't have to look far in Alaska. How is any of this my business?"

"I'm not exactly sure except that. . ." Fiona clamped her mouth shut for a second. She seemed to be thinking again. "Except that when she started telling Merry about how she'd only recently arrived in Skagway in the hopes of finding a husband and starting a family, well. . ."

Tucker had just about lost interest. "Well, what?"

"Well, Merry said that she'd come to the right place."

Now he was interested. "Did my sister say anything else?"

"Just that she ought to come for supper tonight."

Tonight? No, that wouldn't do. He had to figure a way out of this mess before it went any further.

He set his pick down and pressed past Fiona to emerge into the sunshine. Much as he loved his twin sister, he couldn't have her pawning him off to the first marriageable female just because he admitted he felt a little lonely on occasion.

There had to be a way to get out of this without hurting Meredith. He'd never do that.

Blinking to adjust his vision, Tucker started walking toward nowhere in particular. He didn't get far before he realized the Rafferty woman was trailing him.

Whirling around to warn Fiona off, she ran smack into him. He pitched forward, and Fiona scrambled backward. As Tucker regained his footing, Fiona lost hers. Only his quick thinking saved her from hitting the ground. Tucker wrapped his arm around her waist and yanked her against him, so that she now stood upright on solid footing. She also stood in his arms. The two women approaching saw it all.

Tucker looked down into Fiona's eyes, and a plan was born.

He took a step back and smiled. "Fiona Rafferty, what if

I told you I had a solution to both our problems?"

"I'd say I'm interested." Fiona gave him a sideways look. "But I didn't know you had a problem."

He leaned forward and spoke softly into her left ear. "I don't yet, and if you'll follow my lead, maybe I can keep it that way."

"So if I help you, then you'll help me. Is that what you're saying?"

The pair approached, and he could tell from their posture that they had stopped all pretense of having a jolly stroll in the woods. Unless he missed his guess, Meredith and Violet Abrams were on a mission.

"Tucker?" Fiona tugged at his sleeve. "I need to know if you'll help me get to college."

He looked down at Fiona. "I'll do what I can, but I've never lied to my sister or her husband, and I don't intend to start now."

Fiona chewed on the idea a second, then nodded. "Fair enough. The Lord won't bless a venture that's based on lies. So what is it that I need to do?"

"Simple," he said as he leaned closer. "Forgive me when I kiss you."

eight

Fiona opened her mouth to object, then closed it quickly when Tucker aimed his lips toward her cheek. It lasted only a second, but the brush of his lips touched more than her skin. It etched a memory of a dark-haired man and a chaste moment on her heart.

Oh, it was for show, she knew. But somewhere between that moment and the moment their gazes locked, Tucker Smith had become more than just her brother's brother-in-law. Always and forever, he would be the source of her first kiss. Well, almost a kiss, anyway.

And that thought made her madder than a wet hen. She'd dreamed of this moment since girlhood, wondering about the who, when, and why of it over endless hours in the still of the night. Now, with barely any notice, the long-dreamed-of moment had come and gone.

She looked up at Tucker and tried to speak. Her lips, burned by the near miss of a real romantic kiss, refused to move. Funny, but he seemed to be having similar trouble.

He suddenly looked past her and smiled. "Good afternoon, Merry," he said. "Who've you brought with you today?"

Fiona turned to see her brother's wife escorting the neighbor's niece, a pleasant-looking woman with a ready smile, up the hill. As they neared, Meredith's grin split wide.

"Well, hello yourself, Tucker, Fiona."

Flames leaped into Fiona's cheeks as she realized the ladies had seen it all. They had witnessed the whispered conversation and, to her horror, the kiss, as well.

She turned her attention to Tucker, who refused to meet her

gaze. "You knew they would see us," she whispered. "You did that on purpose."

"Smile," he said without looking her way. "Or at least pretend to. You do want out of Alaska, don't you?"

Fiona nodded.

"Then go along for the time being. I promise I'll not disparage your reputation. I'm a gentleman," he said softly. "If I weren't, I'd have stolen a real kiss." He paused to let that sink in. "Trust me."

"You're no gentleman," she whispered. "You threw my perfectly stylish footwear into the river. And you caused my traveling hat to get dunked."

Tucker gave her his complete attention. "Your stylish footwear nearly killed you when it caused you to tumble off the rocks and then fall into the river. As for that hat, well, it needed a good dunking."

She was about to protest, but he placed his forefinger atop her lips. "Fiona, it's not like I left you shoeless. I did buy you a pair of the best sealskin boots the mercantile had to offer. And what you don't know is that I placed a mail order at the Sears Roebuck for a few suitable things you will need for winter. That, I admit, was Merry's idea, but I did think of the boots myself."

"You bought the boots for me? I thought they were yours." She glanced over at the ladies, who seemed deep in conversation. "No wonder they came close to fitting."

Tucker looked pleased. "You needed something appropriate. Is that a thank-you?"

She pretended an irritation she no longer felt. "Considering you sent a fine pair of kid leather boots downriver, I'm not sure a thank-you is in order." She paused to see the ladies draw near. "But under the circumstances, I'm touched that you would be concerned about me."

"Of course I'm concerned." He lifted his gaze toward his

sister and Miss Abrams. "To what do we owe the pleasure?"

Meredith gathered her wits. "I came to introduce Tucker to Miss Abrams." She paused and seemed to be at a loss for words. "But perhaps we've come at an inopportune moment."

Tucker made the first move, reaching for the stranger's hand. "Pleased to meet you, Miss Abrams. Do tell how your uncle is faring."

"Thanks to you," she said without noting Fiona's presence, "my uncle will make a complete recovery." She paused. "I've heard our family owes you a huge debt of gratitude."

Tucker placed his hand on Fiona's shoulder and shook his head. "I believe you heard wrong, ma'am. You see, your uncle's alive thanks to this young lady's cool head and excellent doctoring skills. Without her, he'd never have made it as far as town."

"Yes," Meredith added. "God seems to have gifted our Fiona with the art of healing. I saw your uncle, and forgive me for saying this, but I suspected he might be done for."

The conversation spun off from there, moving from the ailing neighbor to the niece's trip from Skagway. Somewhere along the way, the threesome completely forgot Fiona was present.

Or at least it seemed that way. Until she tried to slip off toward the cabin.

"Leaving so soon, Fiona?" Meredith called. "Won't you wait and accompany Violet and me over to the Abrams place? I'm sure there's plenty to be done before Mr. Abrams returns."

Tucker nodded. "What say I tag along? I bet I can find a thing or two that needs my attention."

Meredith looked up at her brother with a broad smile. "Oh, Tucker, I think you already have."

Thankfully, Tucker did not respond. In fact, he didn't say a word until they threw open the door of the old miner's shack and stepped inside. "I'm going back to fetch the toolbox.

Looks like this place was falling down around his ears."

Truthfully, Fiona only noticed the disarray. She immediately set to work making the tiny makeshift kitchen shine, while the other two ladies tackled the room where Mr. Abrams had both lived and slept. Tucker returned and began hammering, sawing, and generally making noise in the clearing, which drew Ian's attention.

"Need some help?" Ian called.

Tucker set down his hammer and walked toward Ian, but then Fiona felt another set of eyes on her. Turning, she noticed Meredith studying her intently.

Fiona took a deep breath and exhaled slowly, steadying her hands as well as her nerves. "If you don't need any help, I'm going to gather the washing and go over to the river."

Meredith gave her a knowing smile. "Of course," she said.

The urge to set Meredith straight bore hard on her as Fiona trudged toward the door. Once outside, she managed to slip past Tucker unnoticed. Ian, however, stopped hammering to watch her disappear around the side of the cabin. By the time she reached the river, her brother's hammer was back in use.

Fiona endured the rest of the afternoon by forcing her thoughts in one direction. As long as she kept her mind focused on where she would someday be rather than where she was, things went well. The distance from the house helped, as did the frigid waters of the river.

At one point, Fiona noticed Ian and Meredith standing a few yards from the house deep in conversation. Perhaps she was mistaken, but it seemed as though the two of them were talking about her. As quickly as she could, Fiona finished her task and slipped past Tucker once again.

She found Meredith cleaning the room's lone window while Violet Abrams bounced a fussy Douglas on her knee. "The washing's done," she said as she walked over to smile at the baby. "Would you like me to take this little one back home and see if he will sleep better in his own bed?"

Violet gave the baby willingly to Fiona and rose. "Most days I think I want a houseful," she said. "But they are tiring, aren't they?"

Meredith chuckled. "I only wish I'd been prepared for the lack of sleep. Now that he's trying to cut a tooth, it seems as though he never sleeps more than a few hours at a time." She gave Fiona a sheepish look. "Ask Fiona. I'm sure the little prince keeps her awake with his howling."

Fiona giggled. "Only the first night. After that, I learned that a feather pillow and a fur blanket placed over the ears make an effective sound barrier."

As if on cue, Douglas began to cry. "Perhaps you should see if he's hungry, Merry."

A moment later while the baby nursed, Fiona listened to Violet and Meredith chatter on about everything from the unseasonably mild weather to the best way to can vegetables. Outside, she could hear the sound of men working, punctuated occasionally by the call of a bird or the murmur of deep voices.

Not soon enough, the baby had been fed and burped. "He ought to sleep well now," Meredith said as she handed the bundled child over to Fiona. "If he proves to be too much trouble, fetch him back here."

"He'll be fine. If he complains too much, I'll put him to work helping me make supper."

Fiona looked down into the drowsy face of her nephew. She could see the image of his father in the tiny face. A cap of red fuzz completed the picture of a little fellow destined to grow into the substantial shoes of his father. The only signs of his mother on Douglas's face were the perpetual smile—except for during the recent teething episode—and the shape of his chin.

"Let's go for a walk, young Mr. Rafferty, shall we?" She settled the baby into the crook of her arm and tossed his burping cloth over her shoulder. "Tell your mommy good-bye for now."

As Violet waved, Meredith kissed the top of her son's head, then looked up at Fiona. "I'd like to talk to you later, Fiona," she said. "I think it likely you can guess why."

Fiona's heart thumped against her chest, and her gaze fell to the cabin floor. What a can of worms she'd opened by agreeing to Tucker's ludicrous plan. It occurred to her that she didn't even know what that plan was. Further, he'd made no definite promise to help her.

What was I thinking?

"I assure you there's nothing to talk about, Merry. What you saw. . ." She looked up and forced herself to stare at her sister-in-law directly. "Rather, what you think you saw, well, it wasn't what it seemed."

"How do you think it seemed?" Her sister-in-law gave no indication of her feelings on the matter.

"Seemed like you found yourself a husband, Miss Rafferty." Violet grinned. "I don't suppose he has a brother?"

The woman's comment broke the tension between Fiona and Meredith. "Believe me," Meredith said, "as wonderful as my brother is, you wouldn't wish for more like him. One Tucker Smith is plenty."

Fiona glanced out the door and spied the subject of their discussion leaning over the water bucket, dipping himself a drink. Ian stood nearby, obviously waiting his turn at the dipper.

"Yes," Fiona said, "I have to agree with Merry. I think one is definitely more than enough of Tucker Smith. Now, shall we take that walk, Douglas?"

The baby greeted her with a yawn as they slipped out the door and past the conversing men. She'd almost escaped the premises when Ian caught up with her. He spoke to Douglas in the silly manner that parents address infants, then fell silent.

For a good quarter mile, the pair walked in silence. Fiona refused to be the first to speak; the emotions churning inside her wouldn't allow it. Occasionally, Douglas would snuggle against her, but most of the time varied between sleeping and watching his father intently.

"You've got a way with Douglas," Ian finally said. "You'll be a wonderful mother someday."

She allowed the words to settle deep within her heart. With no illusions of ever being gifted of the Lord with children, she had to be satisfied that someone believed she might be good at it.

They reached the bridge, and Ian sent Fiona ahead of him. The baby stayed still as Fiona balanced his weight while crossing the reused logs. Just before they reached the Rafferty cabin, Ian reached for Fiona's arm.

"Lay the baby down so we can chat, Fiona."

"If it's about Tucker, there's no need." She shifted the sleeping infant to her shoulder and rubbed his back to settle him into sleep again. "What Merry thinks she saw is not what was actually happening."

Ian stood his ground and said not a word as Fiona waited for a response. Finally, he pointed toward the door. "Lay the baby down. There's no need to wake him should the conversation become heated."

Fiona complied, taking her time while she made sure Douglas would not awaken. When she returned, Ian was waiting beside the garden.

"I thought I'd pick peas for dinner. What do you think?"

He looked up, and she realized he must not have noticed her. "I'm sorry, what did you say?"

"Peas. For dinner." Fiona knelt beside the cabbage plants and began to pluck at the weeds growing between them. "Never mind. Go ahead and speak your piece, big brother. I'll not be able to persuade you of anything until you've said it all."

Ian heaved a long sigh. "Fiona, for the life of me, I'll never understand why you think you've been exiled."

She looked up quickly. "Because I have."

"Perhaps it may seem that way, but did you ever think our

father might have had good reason to pack your things and move you here? Maybe reasons you will never know."

Giving up the pretense of weeding, Fiona settled back and faced her brother. "I know *this*, Ian Rafferty. If you or Braden wished to go to medical college, Da would rush up here and dance an Irish jig all the way back to Oregon with your suitcases on his back. Because I'm a woman, he refuses to consider that I, too, might make a decent doctor."

"Oh, Fiona, don't you see? There's no doubt you'd make much more than a decent doctor. We've all known since you were a wee babe that you had the gift." He paused. "That's not the trouble."

She blinked back the tears that threatened. *I will not cry.* "Then what, in your estimation, is the trouble?"

"Don't you see, lassie? Da, he wants you to be happy."

"But the only way I'll be happy is if I'm doing the work the Lord has for me. How could I possibly be happy doing anything else?"

Ian took a minute to ponder her question. At least that's what he seemed to be doing. When he dipped his head and pinched the bridge of his nose, Fiona knew for sure.

Finally, he lifted his gaze to meet hers. "Fiona, I don't pretend to know what the Lord's got for you. I do know what our father entrusted me to do, and that was to see to your welfare until such time as a proper husband can be found to take over the job." He paused. "I'm sorry, but that's what Da says, and I have to abide by it."

Fiona's Irish blood began to boil, and she scrambled to her feet. Twice she tried to respond. On the third attempt, she found her voice.

"Ian, who do you listen to, our earthly father or our heavenly Father?"

"That's not fair." Ian rose, fists clenched. "You know the answer to that."

She stomped her foot, not caring that she behaved more like a petulant child than a woman with a legitimate complaint. "Then why aren't you listening to the Lord on this?"

Ian squared his shoulders and peered down at Fiona. His cheeks were as red as his hair, and his eyes blazed with anger. "Because, little sister," he ground out, "it seems as though you're the only one the Lord is telling these things to. He certainly hasn't let me know, and I doubt He's spoken to Da on the matter either."

With that, Ian turned his back to her and headed toward the river. She had to run to catch him. When she reached his side, she grasped his wrist and held on until he stopped.

"Please hear my side of things, Ian." She didn't care if the tears fell. Her brother could think no less of her for crying. "I never said I didn't want all those things. I would love to have a home and family like you. What I said is that I know this is not what God wants for me, at least not now."

"All right." Ian pulled his wrist away. "Fair enough. But if you truly mean what you're saying, why were you cavorting around with Merry's brother today?"

"Cavorting around?" Her pulse jumped. "Is that what Merry told you?"

"Never mind what my wife and I discuss." Ian's voice went menacingly low. "Is it true he kissed you?"

"Much as I wish it were, that's not exactly true," came a voice from behind them.

Fiona whirled around. Tucker strode toward them. "Great. Just what I need. Tucker, go home. I can handle my brother."

"Her brother doesn't need to be handled." Ian pointed to Tucker. "What her brother needs is an explanation. Your sister tells me she saw you and Fiona in an intimate embrace earlier."

"Could I speak to you about that alone, Ian? Man to man?"

"No." Fiona said the word just as Ian gave his permission. "I want to be a part of this conversation," she added.

"No," both men said together.

"Go check on Douglas," Ian said. "It's not good to leave him alone when he's been so fussy."

Fiona wanted to argue, but it would do no good. Instead, she gave her brother and Tucker an I-haven't-said-my-last-word-on-this look and headed for the cabin. Once inside, she checked on the sleeping baby, then watched through the window as the men strolled out of sight over the hill.

"Lord," she whispered, "if I'm wrong about this mission You've given me, would You make it clear to me that I got it wrong? You know I'm hardheaded sometimes, but I really thought You wanted me to be a doctor. I have to admit, though, I sure did feel something when Tucker kissed me. And holding Douglas, well, I could have a half dozen just like him and be happy as can be." She took a deep breath and let it out slowly. "I've never asked You before, Lord, but would You give me some sort of sign as to whether or not I should pursue my dream of being a doctor?"

She leaned against the windowsill and rested her chin in her hands. "One more thing, God. If you want me to stay here, could You perhaps work on Tucker Smith a bit? I can't find too many things wrong with sharing another kiss with him unless You're not agreeable to it."

❧

"I'm going to give you a chance to come clean, Tucker. I've got the highest respect for you, but I want a straight answer about you and my sister."

Tucker swallowed hard. When he had crafted the plan to be left alone by his matchmaking sister, he'd had no idea what sort of trouble he'd be making for both Fiona and himself.

"I have nothing but the most honorable intentions regarding your sister, Ian."

"Then tell me why my wife saw you kissing her. Are you trying to tell me that Merry lied to me?"

"No, never." Tucker held up his hands. "It's just that what she saw wasn't what it looked like."

Ian looked doubtful. "I'm listening."

"When I heard Merry was up to matchmaking, I didn't want any part of it."

"And you figured a woman looking for a man wouldn't be interested in one who was kissing someone else."

"Exactly."

"If I didn't know you better, I'd think you were saying that you took advantage of my sister for your own benefit." He poked Tucker in the chest with his forefinger. "Is that what I'm hearing? Did you take advantage of my sister?"

"No," he said as he stepped back. "I wanted it to look like something was going on so Merry wouldn't force the Abrams woman on me. You see, we recently had a conversation about how I might be feeling a little lonely now that you two are. . . well. . .never mind."

Ian's expression softened. "So my wife took it upon herself to fix your problem with the first female who wandered up?" When Tucker nodded, Ian burst into a fit of laughter.

"What's so funny?"

"I was about to punch you for taking advantage of my sister and courting her without my permission, and it turns out to be a game you and Fiona played to throw Merry off the chase."

Tucker joined in the laughter, but a tiny part of his heart refused to go along with the joke. That little sliver of warmth nestled against the cold loneliness he'd felt since his sister married off kept him from declaring victory.

Rather, he had a sinking feeling he hadn't shared his last kiss with Fiona Rafferty. And that feeling scared him more than anything.

nine

Ian must have been satisfied with whatever Tucker said, because nothing further was mentioned of the great kiss-by-the-tree debacle. Over the next week, Tucker returned to his pattern of working long hours at the stake and spending what little free time he had at the Rafferty cabin. Eventually, Fiona got used to ignoring the fact that the man sitting on the other side of the table was the same man whose lips had brushed her cheek.

Then she found herself with Tucker after dinner, taking a meal to Mr. Abrams and his niece. By the time they reached the Abramses' cabin, Fiona still hadn't figured out how she had ended up alone on this mission with Tucker. If he had anything to say about it, he kept his peace, speaking only when Violet answered the door.

"We brought supper for the two of you," Tucker said. "It's good to see you back home, Mr. Abrams."

The older man nodded and expressed his thanks while Violet dished the food out and began to feed her uncle. After spending another half hour visiting, Fiona and Tucker made their getaway.

Strolling back under a cloudless sky, Fiona couldn't help but smile. At least she couldn't complain about the Alaskan summer. The long days had been a burden to bear for a while, but now that she'd grown accustomed to sleeping by the clock rather than the light, things went much smoother.

Then there was the friendship that had developed between her and Tucker. It all started when she took to wearing the boots he'd bought her. She found them surprisingly comfortable, and being warm and waterproof made them even better.

The first time Tucker saw her in them, he smiled. He'd been doing so ever since. Oddly, being around Tucker had begun to make her smile, too.

"Penny for your thoughts."

She looked up at the object of her thoughts. "Not on your life, Tucker. I'm never telling."

"Oh? Is that right? Well, I have my ways and. . ."

Fiona stopped midway across the bridge and looked down into the clear river. Several decent-sized frying fish teased her from their watery home. How long had it been since she'd gone fishing? Too long.

"Fiona, are you listening to me?"

"Hmm? I'm sorry. What did you say? I was thinking about fishing."

Tucker gave her an incredulous look.

She held her hands up in a defensive pose. "I'm sorry. I know it was rude. It's just that all my life I've been my father's fishing buddy. Neither of my brothers cared for it, and Da said I was a quick study. As long as I can remember I've had a fishing pole in my hand." She paused. "At least I did until I came here. I didn't realize until just now how very much I miss it."

Silence.

"Tucker?" Fiona said. "Do you realize you're staring at me?"

He nodded.

"Well, stop it." She turned her back and headed toward the cabin, stopping only when she realized Tucker hadn't kept up. "Tucker Smith, get off the bridge and go home. I don't know what's gotten into you, but you are acting silly."

He caught up with her a moment later. "You're serious, aren't you?"

"About what, Tucker?" Fiona stopped to peer up at him. "Is something wrong with you? I don't think I've ever seen you acting so odd. Well, other than on the trip back from town."

"I'm sorry." He scrubbed his face with the palms of his hands. "Did you just say you like to fish?"

"Yes," she said slowly. "Is there something wrong with that?"

❧

"Wrong?" Tucker's laugh echoed against the nearby hills. "No," he said as he grabbed her by the waist and began to swing her around. "That's wonderful." He set her down, then had to steady her when she wobbled a bit.

"Tucker Smith, what's gotten into you?" She primped her hair until she'd smoothed it back into place.

He had to tame his smile to get a word out. "Fiona, I've been living here for nigh on three years, and not once during that time did I ever have anyone to go fishing with. Your brothers are good men, but neither of them has the patience it takes to wait out a decent-sized fish."

She nodded. "That's true."

"Now, mind you, a man likes to fish alone most of the time, but on occasion, it's a fine thing to have someone else to compare your catch with. Outside of the good Lord and a hot cup of black coffee, that's about my favorite thing." He paused to give her a sideways look. "Now *you're* looking at *me* funny. Did I say something wrong?"

Fiona took a deep breath and let it out slowly. "Nothing, really. It's just that, well, I feel the same way."

Tucker eyed the redhead and waited for her to say the punch line. Surely someone as pretty and smart as this one had other things to do than fish.

Then came the absurd question of whether she wore that silly hat and those impractical shoes to fish in. Well, it couldn't be possible.

Maybe he ought to call her bluff. Yes, that idea definitely had appeal.

He affected a casual pose. "So, Fiona," he said as he studied the distance, "what say you and I go fishing after Sunday dinner?" Tucker paused for effect. "Of course, if you're busy, I'll understand."

"Too busy to fish?" She shook her head. "Anyone too busy to fish is just plain too busy. You bring the bait, and I'll fix the coffee."

❧

On the appointed day, Tucker had the bait packed and ready in the bucket when he arrived at the Rafferty place for their weekly Sunday services. Fiona looked pretty as ever. Evidently, she had more than one pair of those ridiculous shoes, because the ones she wore with her flowered dress looked just like the ones he'd sent downriver.

He felt a little bad about doing that, but only a little. Still, he shouldn't have tossed the shoes.

"I'll just be a minute," she said as she headed for the kitchen once the services were over. "Do you have a spot in mind?"

Ian looked up from his reading while Meredith watched Tucker from the corner where she held the sleeping baby. Neither spoke, but then they didn't need words to show their curiosity.

"Fishing," Tucker felt compelled to say. "Fiona loves to fish. I just found this out."

"I see," Ian responded curtly, although Tucker thought he might have detected the slightest hint of a grin.

Never had Tucker felt so out of place in his sister's home. "I'll just wait outside," he said as he backed out, running into the doorframe in the process.

Sitting on a tree stump and waiting for Fiona, Tucker frowned. "What's wrong with me? It's just fishing. Why, those two act like I've come courting."

"What did you say?"

He looked up. Fiona headed his way with a basket. She wore a pretty flowered dress, a fairly sensible hat with a straw brim encircled by a black ribbon, and the sealskin boots he'd bought for her. To his surprise, she carried her own pole along with the basket.

"Did you bring worms, too?" He gestured to the basket. "I thought I told you I would take care of that."

Her laughter made him smile. "No, it's not worms. Fishing's not fishing without coffee and snacks," she said. "I don't know if I mentioned it, but when I start fishing, I generally stay all day." She stopped short and gave him an appraising look.

"What?" he asked. "Did I do something wrong?"

"Not yet," she said, "but I wonder if you're one of those fellows who likes to talk while he fishes. If you are, I should warn you that we won't be sitting near one another. I like to do my fishing in silence. It's the best time to talk to the Lord, you know. And besides," she said with a wink, "talking scares the fish away." Her expression turned serious. "Unless you like to talk while you fish. I surely don't mean to suggest that —"

"No, it's quite all right. I believe I can abide by the no-talking rule. One question, though."

She set the basket down to adjust her hat. "What's that?"

"Does the no-talking rule apply to snack times? I mean, a fellow might find himself in trouble if he asks someone to pass the salt, so I feel we should spell out the rules beforehand."

Fiona pretended to think hard. "No, I believe talking is allowed during snack times."

Tucker reached for the basket's handle. "All right, then. Let's go fishing."

"Yes, let's. Where are the big ones biting?"

He answered by pointing south. As she walked ahead in that direction, Tucker suppressed a groan, and he turned to a prayer of his own to save him.

Over the course of the afternoon, his fears grew. Not only did Fiona Rafferty know her way around a fishing pole, but she also caught more fish than he had and even offered to bait his hook. It was a side of the redhead that both intrigued and terrified him.

And Tucker Smith didn't scare easily.

For the first time since he had left Texas, he was enjoying himself with a woman who was not his relative. Tucker set his pole into the soft dirt and leaned back on his elbows. Some twenty yards downriver, Fiona was reeling in a good-sized Dolly Varden.

He watched her drop the fish into a bucket that was nearly brimming already. Without missing a beat, she reached over and jabbed the hook into an unsuspecting worm, then cast the freshly baited hook out in a perfect arc toward midstream.

Lord, I'm in trouble. I think I could actually fall in love with this one.

Two hours into their fishing trip, Tucker called a time-out for coffee. To his surprise, Fiona willingly obliged, and soon they were sitting side by side, swapping fish tales about the ones that got away.

When the conversation slowed, Tucker sipped at his coffee and watched his companion as she lay back to look up at the clouds.

"Look, it's a rabbit." She pointed straight up, and when Tucker tried to follow her gaze, he nearly fell over.

"Looks more like a dog to me," he said. "See the tail?"

"That's not the tail, Tucker." She giggled. "That's the ears."

They lapsed into companionable silence, only speaking when the look of a particular cloud needed to be debated. When the silence went on too long, Tucker closed his eyes and let the sun warm his face while his breathing slowed.

"I could get used to this." Tucker opened his eyes and looked over at Fiona, who was no longer at his side. To his surprise, she'd just cast her hook into the river near the bank. "I said that out loud, didn't I?"

To her credit, Fiona shrugged. "I'm fishing. There's no talking in fishing, remember?"

With a chuckle, Tucker closed his eyes and resumed his

contemplation of the backs of his eyelids until he reached a state where he could still hear the sounds of the river but he no longer noticed anything else. His sleep was light, barely below wakefulness lest Fiona should need him.

Fiona. He thought of her as he lay there, of his own reasons for escaping this corner of Alaska, and then let his thoughts drift to why he was there in the first place. He'd been running when he got here, and if he headed out with the Harriman folks, he'd still be running.

He'd already lost his past and a good woman to his running. Did he really want to keep it up?

Somewhere during that nap, Tucker gave up all pretense of wanting to leave Alaska, even for a brief time. The Harriman Expedition would do just fine without him. Experienced guides were a dime a dozen in this part of the country.

Women like Fiona Rafferty, however, were not. That realization almost caused him to sit up and smile.

Almost, but not quite. He did feel quite comfortable lying here.

"What did you want to be when you grew up, Tucker?"

The sound of her voice startled him, and he had to gather his wits. He also had to force his eyes to open, but what he saw was worth the effort.

Fiona sat beside him again, a cup of coffee in her hand and the bucket full of wriggling fish. She'd set aside her proper straw hat and captured that fiery hair of hers into a knot.

She scooted closer to lean her back against the tree, ankles crossed, then sat in silence, never pushing him for an answer. She seemed confident she would have one eventually.

Tucker rolled over on his side and supported himself on one elbow. "I don't think I've ever told anyone this, not even Merry." He paused. "You have to promise two things before I will tell you."

"Sounds serious."

"It's very serious. I'm not a man who shares his secrets with just anyone."

Fiona gave him a look of mock horror as she pressed her palms to her cheeks. "Oh, I don't know, Tucker. I'm not sure I'm fit to take on this responsibility."

"Very funny. How old are you?"

"Nineteen." She tucked a loose tendril behind her ear and reached for the hat, setting it on just so. "Why?"

He shrugged. "No reason, I suppose. I just wondered."

"I could ask how old you are, but I'm more interested in this deep, dark secret of yours."

"Twenty-three," he said. "And as for the deep, dark secret, well, I always wanted to follow in my father's footsteps. He was a railroad man. I've dreamed of it since childhood. Do you find that odd?"

Tucker waited for Fiona to laugh. When she didn't, his estimation of her soared.

She seemed to be cogitating on his statement, so he left her to it. Picking up his pole, he urged the line back onto shore and stabbed another worm onto the hook.

"Some fisherman you are," she said with a grin. "You slept through a good-sized trout."

He pretended disgust. "Some fisherman you are. You allowed a good-sized trout to help itself to a feast without getting caught."

"I am a fisher*woman*, thank you very much." Fiona stuck her nose in the air, and her hat tumbled back off her head. She ignored it to give the line her attention.

"Fisherwoman it is." He cast his line out into midstream and watched the hook sink with a satisfying *plop*. "But what excuse do you offer for letting a perfectly decent fish get away?"

Fiona yanked at the line, then glanced over at Tucker. "I assumed that since you had no intention of catching him, the least I could do was let the fish eat something so he could get a little bigger before I landed him."

And so they bantered, he about her inconsiderate nature and she about his casual attitude toward fishing. By the time hunger pangs hit, the second bucket was full, and their catch was enough for twice the number of diners at the supper table.

"I suppose we should take these back and clean them," Fiona said. "It'll be supper soon enough."

"Grab the poles and the basket, and I'll take these." Tucker reached for both buckets and turned toward the cabin. "Oh. I should have told you before we left that the rule around here is whoever catches them cleans them."

Fiona looked him in the eye and nodded before hoisting the poles onto her shoulder. "Of course."

They were almost in sight of the cabin when Tucker stopped short. "Fiona," he said, "I had a great time."

For the first time that afternoon, the redhead looked shy. "So did I."

"We should do this again next Sunday."

She agreed quickly. Then her cheeks blazed. "That is," she added as she looked away, "if Mercy doesn't have need of me."

Setting the buckets down, Tucker stared down into eyes he only now realized were the deep green of fresh clover. "Of course," he somehow managed to say.

"And if the weather's nice."

He moved an inch closer. Close enough to count every freckle on her nose. "Definitely," he said.

"Next Sunday, it is," she said as she pressed past him to snag the buckets and march toward the cabin.

Tucker couldn't decide whether he'd just missed out on something wonderful or had just missed landing in a boatload of trouble. As he watched the redhead sharpening the knife that would clean the fish, he decided the answer was a little of both.

ten

For the next three Sundays, Meredith had no need for Fiona, and Tucker managed to join the Raffertys for every meal, breaking his usual habit of only showing up for supper. Never did he seem to mind Ian's ribbing or Meredith's gentle questioning, although he remained steadfastly silent on his renewed interest in family gatherings.

Fiona would have had to be blind to miss the fact that Tucker seemed to be paying more than the usual amount of attention to her. For her part, Fiona feared she might be falling in love—something she dared not do, considering the short amount of time she had left in Goose Chase.

Each time she left the cabin and headed toward the river with Tucker, Fiona couldn't help but smile. Unlike other times, however, today Tucker seemed preoccupied.

At first Fiona ignored him, calculating that whatever ailed the man would soon be set aside in favor of an afternoon of good fishing and even better coffee. Then he had the audacity to complain about the coffee.

"That does it." Fiona stood. "If you can't be decent company, then why don't you try being quiet? Remember, there's no talking when you're fishing."

Tucker's look quickly faded. "All right," he said. "You want company? I'll give you company and talking. I was just wondering if your letter was from the medical college."

Stunned, she asked, "How did you know I got a letter?"

"Because I was with Ian when Braden brought the mail from town." He crossed his arms over his chest. "The one on top of the stack had your name on it."

Her brothers had noticed, too, but they were obviously waiting for her to bring it up. It would have been hard to miss the look Ian gave her when he handed her the envelope. Surely he and Braden had discussed what it might contain.

Fiona hadn't decided exactly what she would say if asked, but she knew she couldn't lie. She also knew she had to be in Oregon when the term began, and according to the letter, that only gave her two more Sundays to fish before she had to leave Goose Chase.

Two more Sundays with the man she'd somehow fallen in love with.

Thinking about it just made things worse, so she decided to lighten the mood. "So you're brooding over the fact I got a letter?" She feigned a playful smile. "Why, Tucker Smith, are you jealous?"

The joke did not have its intended effect. Rather, Tucker stood and dusted off his trousers. Without saying a word, he grabbed the half-filled buckets and stalked away.

Fiona opened her mouth to comment, then thought better of it and went back to fishing. If she caught anything, she'd just carry the fish home wrapped in her apron.

She felt a tug on the line and watched as the granddaddy of all trout nibbled at the bait on her hook.

"Fisherwoman, what excuse do you offer for letting a perfectly decent fish get away?"

She didn't have to turn around to know Tucker was walking toward her. "I assumed that since you had no intentions of catching him, the least I could do was let the fish eat something so he could get a little bigger before I landed him."

He came around to stand between her and the river. Somewhere along the way, he'd set aside the buckets, for now his hands were empty.

"I'm going to speak my piece, Fiona, and I don't want you to say a thing. Nod if you understand." When she complied, he continued. "All right, I'm just going to come right out and say it. These last few weeks have, well, they've given me a lot to think about."

Fiona wanted to speak, wanted to say she, too, had found plenty to consider. Instead, she settled for another nod.

"It all comes down to this. Fiona Rafferty, somewhere between the coffee and the fishing, I've fallen in love with you." He began to pace, and Fiona tried her best to keep her focus on him. "Yes, that's right, I have fallen in love. I know it may surprise you, but—"

"No, it doesn't." Fiona smiled. "I've fallen in love with you, too, Tucker."

He stopped his pacing and whirled around. "I'm serious, Fiona. Don't joke with me."

Tears stung her eyes, and she blinked them away. "I'm serious, too. I can't account for it, but I'm ready to admit I'm in love with you." She shook her head. "There's just one problem."

Tucker looked stricken. "What's that?"

"You haven't asked me to stay yet."

"I can remedy that problem right now." He crossed the distance between them to encircle her wrist with his fingers. Lifting her hand to his lips, he softly kissed her knuckles as he met her gaze. "I want to do this right and proper, so I'm going to speak to your brothers since your father isn't here. I just want to be completely sure of one thing first."

Fiona's tears fell as she contemplated the importance of this conversation. She knew what he was going to ask, but rather than answer, she let him speak the words first. "What's that?"

"I've known since we met at that fishing vessel in Goose Chase that you never meant to make this place your home. Can you give up medicine to be a wife to me?"

She took only a moment to consider what Tucker asked. Her heart soared as she whispered, "Yes."

Tucker's yelp of happiness was probably heard all the way

back at the cabin. He lifted Fiona by the waist and swung her around, then held her against him and kissed the top of her head. "You've made me the happiest man in Alaska, Fiona Rafferty. If you have no objections, I'd like to go back to the cabin and let Merry and Ian know."

Fiona looked up into the eyes of the man she loved and tried to nod. Tears blurred his handsome face and rendered her useless until Tucker wiped them away with his handkerchief.

"Would it be too forward of me to steal a kiss?"

Fiona smiled. "Why, is Violet Abrams headed this way?"

"If she is, then she'd best close her eyes else she's going to see the best kiss ever given on Alaskan soil." With that, he made good on his promise.

"Tucker," Fiona whispered some moments later. "Do you suppose you can top that kiss?"

Tucker leaned down and cradled her cheek with the palm of his hand. "I might, darlin', but not until we're married. I'm sure it will be worth the wait, though."

The walk back to the cabin took forever. Of course, it didn't help that every few feet she had to stop and look at Tucker to see if she'd dreamed the whole thing. They got all the way to the clearing before Tucker realized he had left the fish back at the river.

"You go on inside, but don't you dare say a word. I want to speak to Ian before you go blabbing, you hear?"

"I might be convinced, but it will take another kiss."

Tucker complied, then sent her toward the door. "Not a word, now," he said as he hurried back toward the river.

Fiona took a moment to compose herself, first by breathing deeply, then by making sure her hair was fixed just so and the tears she'd shed were no longer evident. Just when she thought her nerves had calmed, a male voice called her name, and she nearly jumped out of her skin.

"Mr. Wily," she said as the man rounded the corner of the

cabin. "Did you bring mail?"

He nodded. "That and company."

"We have company?" She accepted the packet of letters from Wily, then strained to see inside the cabin. "Who is he?"

Wily scratched his head and shrugged. "Don't rightly know, except that he's a she."

Fiona held the letters to her chest and strolled toward the cabin door. The sound of voices drifted toward her, two female and the other decidedly male. Ian and Meredith had company, but who?

She took a deep breath and said a prayer that she could get through visiting with strangers without giving away her secret. The precious secret she shared with Tucker Smith.

"Fiona, I didn't expect you back so soon."

As her eyes adjusted to the dimness of the room, she found Meredith and offered her a smile. Ian sat some distance away, and if she didn't know better, Fiona would think her brother was royally irritated.

"Dear," Ian said, "why don't you introduce Fiona to our guest?"

Meredith looked flustered. A woman—the one she thought was Violet—dressed in a traveling suit of fine navy wool and matching hat sat across the table from her. The woman's face beamed, and her smile revealed perfect teeth framed by full, red lips.

"I'm Elizabeth," the elegant woman said. "Elizabeth Bentley."

"This is my sister, Fiona," Ian supplied.

Elizabeth reached out to place a gloved hand atop Meredith's. "I want to thank you for your letter. I must say I never expected to hear from you." She paused. "From either of you, actually."

"Yes, well, about that letter." Meredith swallowed hard and cast a furtive glance at Fiona. "You see, that letter was written months ago. Ages, really. I thought that Tucker—"

"Thought Tucker what?"

Fiona turned to see her soon-to-be husband standing in the

door. She offered him a smile, but he looked right past her. "Tucker?"

No response. She tried again as he stepped into a shaft of daylight. Still he did not respond.

What Fiona saw on his face, however, frightened her. In the span of half a second, the man she loved had completely forgotten she was in the room.

"Elizabeth?" His voice trembled as he said the woman's name. "What are you doing here?"

"Merry sent her a letter." Ian rose. "She thought you might be. . ." Ian looked over at Fiona with an unreadable expression. "Never mind, I'm going to take our son out for some fresh air. I'll be outside with Wily if anyone needs me." With that, he gathered a sleeping Douglas from his resting spot and pressed past Fiona to head out the door. "Let me rephrase that," he said. "Fiona, I will be outside with Wily when you need me."

An uncomfortable silence descended, and Fiona got the impression she was the only one in the room without the full story. "Someone tell me what's going on here," she said.

"Tucker," Elizabeth said, "you look as handsome as ever."

Tucker remained frozen and mute. The color had drained from his face, and he looked as though he'd seen a ghost. Meredith didn't look much better.

Elizabeth rose and removed her gloves, setting them on the table and arranging them just so. Then she made her way across the room and came to stand close to Tucker. Far too close, in Fiona's estimation, although Tucker did nothing to move away.

Or maybe he didn't notice. His eyes seemed glazed over, and he looked as if anything other than breathing could be accomplished only with great effort.

"Tucker," Fiona said, "what's going on here?"

For a moment, Tucker's vision seemed to clear. He looked at Fiona. "I'm sorry," came out in a strangled reply. "I'm so very sorry."

"Don't be silly." Elizabeth tapped Tucker on the shoulder, then let her hand linger there a bit too long for Fiona's comfort. "You're acting as if you're not glad to see me. I know better than that, Tucker Smith. What I don't know is why you didn't write me to tell me that yourself."

"Where you want these, miss?" Wily stood in the doorway with a set of matched valises balanced on one shoulder.

Elizabeth turned to Meredith. "Where am I staying?" She aimed a broad smile at Tucker. "Just for two nights, of course. My father's expecting us in Goose Chase day after tomorrow."

"*Us?*"

Something was wrong. If only Fiona could put her finger on it. Tucker and Meredith were still staring at Elizabeth, and the houseguest was making eyes at Fiona's fiancé while saying her father was waiting to see Tucker and his sister back in town.

Fiona turned to him. "Tucker, maybe this would be a good time to speak to Ian." When he gave her a blank look, she continued. "You know, about that thing you and I discussed at the river?"

His eyes blinked, but otherwise Tucker continued to stand stock-still as a deep red flushed his cheeks. His fists, she noticed, were clenched, as was his jaw. When she touched Tucker's sleeve, he jerked away, then looked down and met her gaze.

"I'm sorry, Fiona." He turned his attention to the visitor. "I thought my obligations had been released."

Fiona heard the words, but their meaning refused to sink in. She reached for the nearest thing—Tucker's arm—to steady herself.

"*Obligations?* Well, Tucker, I don't know what's gotten into you." The stranger turned to Meredith. "I declare, I don't remember him acting this way back in Texas. Do you, Merry? I don't believe he ever referred to me as an *obligation*. Are you really doing that now, Tucker, or was that just an unfortunate choice of words?"

"Elizabeth," Meredith said slowly, "I'm not sure how to tell you this, but certain situations may have changed since I wrote you."

"You. . .wrote. . .to. . .her?" Tucker paused to shake his head. "That explains why she's here, but why did you do it, Merry?"

"You were lonely, Tucker." Meredith took a step toward her brother, then seemed to think better of it. "Remember when we talked about how God had blessed me with Ian and Douglas? I wanted you to be happy again. It seems so long ago now. I thought maybe. . ."

"You thought maybe what?" Elizabeth turned to Tucker. "You and I are affianced, Tucker. You and my father may have agreed that due to your father's unfortunate reverses, my reputation would best be saved by ending our association until your fortunes changed, but I don't recall you saying that to me. Do you?"

"Affianced?" Fiona clutched Tucker's arm tight enough to leave a mark while she waited for him to tell the awful woman to leave. Instead, he slid from her grasp.

The room began to spin. Tucker's face went out of focus, but his voice was clear.

"No," Tucker said, "I was afraid to see you alone. Afraid I couldn't leave you like I promised."

"Well, now, you never need fear losing me again." She cast a glance around the cabin. "It certainly looks as though your fortunes have improved, and I know you've made good on your father's unfortunate setbacks." Elizabeth smiled at Meredith. "It's the talk of the town that the Smith family name has been cleared. We all assumed the gold in Alaska had been found in great abundance on the Smith properties."

"Tucker." Fiona sighed weakly as she battled to keep her last meal from making a reappearance on Meredith's clean floor. "Tell her." She looked up into his eyes and saw only sadness. "Please," she managed.

"My father is waiting in Goose Chase for us, Tucker." Elizabeth's voice wavered. "I didn't come here on my own. I was invited." She paused to meet Fiona's stare before turning back to Tucker. "You promised yourself to me, and I to you. True, our plans were interrupted due to financial reversals, but that situation has been remedied." Her voice inched an octave lower. "I thought you were an honorable man."

"An honorable woman would keep her promises, Elizabeth."

Fiona swayed, and Tucker steadied her. Meredith stepped toward her, but Fiona waved her away.

Elizabeth's face flushed bright red. "Whatever are you insinuating, Tucker?"

"I am insinuating nothing, Elizabeth." He cleared his throat and seemed to find his voice. "I received a letter from our mutual friend John Worthington a few weeks ago, thanking me for paying my father's debts. In it, our friend mentioned keeping company with my former fiancée. I passed the statement off as a taunt not worth answering." He paused. "Perhaps it was a warning."

The woman seemed unable to speak. A bright flush crept up her neck and settled in crimson stains atop her prominent cheekbones. "Why, the nerve of. . .the unmitigated. . ."

"Elizabeth," he interrupted, "I am a man of my word." He paused to square his shoulders. "If we are truly still affianced, you would not be keeping company with the town banker."

"Dear Elizabeth, let me help you decide where to put your things." Meredith reached for Elizabeth's elbow and led her out the door. "Mr. Wily, join us outside, please. I believe my brother has a bit of business to take care of, and I would love to show Miss Elizabeth more of our lovely place."

As she passed, her eyes pleaded with her brother; then her gaze landed on Fiona. "I didn't know," she whispered.

Elizabeth ignored the scene unfolding around her and offered Tucker a smile before disappearing outside. "What a lovely place you have here, Merry," echoed through the open door as their footsteps receded. "I had no idea Alaska could be so beautiful."

"Tucker, say something. Didn't you just make the same promise to me?"

He let out a long breath and dropped into the nearest chair, scrubbing his face with his palms as he studied the floor. An eternity later, he looked into her eyes. "Yes," he said slowly, "but I promised her first."

"You promised her *first*?" The words emerged, but her feelings remained numb, stuck somewhere between disbelief and disgust. "First?"

Fiona's nails dug into her palms, and she tightened her fingers into fists. If only she were a man. Then she could slug Tucker and be done with it.

No, she decided as she forced herself to breathe again. She would never be done with this.

Ever.

"Fiona, please say something."

Tucker's pleading look left Fiona cold. If her feet weren't rooted to the floor, she might have run. Instead she stood still and watched the room spin.

"I love you, Fiona, but I have to honor the promise I made." He rose and took a step toward her. "I thought she didn't want me anymore. I thought —no, I was certain I had been released from my obligation to marry her."

Fiona found her voice and her anger. "But now you've decided you haven't been?"

"It's obvious I am not free to choose you." His anguished whisper did not move her.

"Then you and I have nothing further to discuss."

Without sparing Tucker Smith so much as a glance, Fiona calmly packed what she could carry and walked out into the Alaskan sunshine. Three steps from the cabin door, she went numb altogether, a merciful respite from the feelings formerly battling for release.

A quick glance back revealed Tucker standing in the doorway. "Fiona, please," he said.

She stopped short and whirled around. "Please what? Please stay?"

A stricken look crossed his face. "I can't ask that of you."

"No," she said as she tightened her grip on her bag, "you can't, can you?" Another moment and she might have run back to him, so Fiona turned away.

Just over the rise, she spied Mr. Wily and called to him. He nodded and loped over to relieve her of some of her luggage.

"You'll be fine, miss," he said, and Fiona noted his face showed neither surprise nor sympathy.

"I will, won't I?" she said to his retreating back.

"What's going on here?" Ian called. "It looks as if you're leaving."

Fiona met Ian on the way to the river and kissed her brother and nephew good-bye. "It's time for me to go."

He seemed to be at a loss for words. Fiona decided to help him with an explanation.

"It seems as though there's one too many women here, big brother," she said. "You really ought to go up and get to know Tucker's fiancée. She's quite lovely."

"Tucker's what?" He shook his head. "I thought you and he, well. . .surely you misunderstood. That was in the past."

"Perhaps Tucker misunderstood, because it seems as though he is still affianced to Elizabeth."

Mr. Wily approached, and Fiona handed him the rest of her bags. She waited until he disappeared before continuing her conversation with Ian.

"Now, I hate to keep Mr. Wily waiting, Ian, but I do want to talk about one more thing. Da will not be happy about my leaving so soon."

He shook his head. "Fiona, I'm more worried about what *you're* unhappy about. Please just come back to the house, and let's talk about this. There must be an explanation for whatever you think you've seen."

"I know what I saw." She looked past him to the sky, now a brilliant blue. "You're not going to try and stop me, are you, Ian?"

Ian entwined his fingers with hers, and she glanced back at him balancing the sleeping baby on his opposite shoulder. "Let one of us go with you, Fiona. It's not safe for a woman to travel alone."

"Thank you, but Mr. Wily will see me to Goose Chase. Doc Killbone told me he'd be sure I got to Oregon in time for school if that was what I wanted to do." Fiona looked her brother in the eyes and tried to hold her tears at bay. "I'll help the doctor at the clinic until he can secure passage for me."

Ian looked worried. "Braden and I will come into Goose Chase to see you off. Would that be all right?"

Fiona kissed the top of the baby's head, then did the same on her brother's cheek. "That would be fine, Ian, but it's not necessary."

"I didn't ask if it was necessary." Douglas raised his head, then cuddled against Ian's neck, eyes half closed. "Besides," Ian said softly, "you'll need the rest of your things. If the weather's nice, we'll bring Douglas and the wives and make it a real family send-off."

"All right. I'll take a room at the boardinghouse next door to the doctor's office. It's safe and clean, and the rooms aren't expensive."

"Yes, I know the place." He seemed to be studying her or perhaps trying to think of something to say.

Unable to remain under her brother's scrutiny, Fiona stepped away and glanced over at the river where Wily stood waiting. "Tell Merry I love her. I don't hold this against her," she said.

"And tell her I would like it very much if she supported her brother in his upcoming marriage but never mentioned anything to me of the details."

Ian considered the request before saying, "I think you ought to tell her yourself."

"I will," she said slowly, "but not today. I just can't."

"Fair enough," Ian said. "What should I tell Tucker?"

"Tucker who?"

eleven

The trip downriver to Goose Chase seemed to happen in a fog. As was his habit, Mr. Wily said only a few words. He did occasionally nod or shake his head, leaving Fiona to wonder whether he was offering an opinion on the day's events or thinking of something else altogether.

When they reached Goose Chase, she watched Mr. Wily scurry past with her bags. "Where are you going?" she called.

"Boardinghouse," was his curt response.

"Of course."

She followed in a numb state and allowed herself to be led to a small suite on the front corner of the rooming house by the elderly proprietor. As soon as the woman left, Fiona crossed the compact parlor to the bedroom and shut the door behind her. Exhaustion sifted through her like heavy sand, and she lay back on the narrow bed.

"What happened, Lord? I was so happy. Was that just this afternoon?" Tears welled, but she closed her eyes against them. "Or was it a lifetime ago?"

Fiona gave herself over to sleep so deep that she had difficulty awakening. Was it a nap or a night's worth of slumber? The sun shining high in the sky gave no clue, nor did the tiredness in her bones.

This time of year, the sun dipped below the horizon for minutes, not hours, and even then darkness never quite came. To think she might have considered living the rest of her life under such conditions.

Sighing, Fiona let her eyes droop once more. She tried to pray, but much as she wanted to, she could not get beyond the question of why God allowed her happiness to be so short lived. Da would remind her that happiness is never guaranteed, but for the moment, she didn't care to hear it.

"To be truthful, I never *did* care to hear it," she said with a chuckle. "Oh, Da, what will I be telling you about this escapade of mine?"

A knock at the door startled her, and she sat bolt upright, her head swimming. "Yes?" she managed as she smoothed her hair.

"You've got a visitor, miss," the proprietor said.

Fiona's heart leaped. Tucker had come for her. She climbed to her feet. "Tell Mr. Smith I'll be right down."

"No, miss," she said. "It's the doctor to see you down in the parlor. Doc Killbone, that is."

Fiona swallowed her disappointment, then walked to the bowl and pitcher. "Tell him I'll be down directly, please."

The image that met Fiona across the basin was a stranger. She quickly averted her gaze and poured water into the basin. Her face washed and hair combed and neatly tucked into a braid, she descended the stairs to meet the town doctor.

"Forgive me for making you wait, Dr. Killbone," she said as she shook his hand.

"Nonsense, dear." The doctor studied her much the same as Ian had only yesterday. Or was it the day before? "When Mr. Wily delivered your brother's note, I must say I was surprised. I had to come and see for myself that you'd actually decided to take me up on my offer to see to your safe passage to medical school. That is why you're here, isn't it?"

She nodded her head. "Yes, absolutely. Did you say my brother sent you a note?"

"Yes, indeed." The doctor patted his front pocket. "Short and sweet it was. Asked me to see to your safety and to send word if he didn't make it to town before you left."

"But how?" She shook her head. "How did Ian send a note?"

"Oh, it weren't Ian. Braden's the one who sent the note."

He smiled. "I can see you're confused. It seems as though Mr. Wily ran into Braden on the way out with the woman from Texas. I guess your brother figured you'd be heading for the hills when he found out who Wily was carrying upstream."

"So Braden knew?" Her eyes narrowed. "And you know. Who else knows about my humiliation?"

"There, there, now," the doctor said. "Goose Chase is a small town, I'll give you that, but we're private people. We don't cotton to disparaging words being said about our own."

"Our own," she repeated. "Funny how I didn't feel like I belonged until I had to make the choice to stay or go. I certainly don't pretend to understand what the Lord's planning now."

Doc Killbone crossed his arms over his chest. "Oh, I don't know, Miss Rafferty. Perhaps the Lord is merely guiding you away in order to prepare you for your return." He paused. "Now tell me, Fiona Rafferty, are you certain you want to take those folks at the college up on their offer to educate you in medicine?"

Was she? "Sure as I can be right now," she answered honestly.

Again he studied her. Then he slowly began to nod. "Fair enough. In that case, I believe I can recommend a suitable escort and a ship heading south."

"Escort?" Fiona shook her head. "I came here alone, and I can certainly go home the same way."

"Dear, if I recall, the reverend and his wife sent you forth from Skagway under the supervision of Mrs. Minter's brother, the ship's captain." His brows shot up. "I rarely forget these things."

"Yes, that's true," she said. "It seems so long ago I nearly forgot."

"Time passes quickly, I've found, when we are most happy. I warrant you will blink and find medical college has ended." He smiled. "Rarely do I find someone so well suited to the trade. Now don't forget your promise to come back here and help me someday."

"I won't forget," she said, "but I wonder if I might ask one favor from you."

He gave her a sideways glance. "What's that, dear?"

"Might you write my da? He's going to be awful upset when he finds out what I've done. I wonder if you might tell him what you've told me about my aptitude for the healing arts."

Dr. Killbone considered her words. At last, he nodded. "Of course, I'd be happy to do that. Why, if I had a daughter, I would be proud if she turned out like you."

She almost cried. Instead, she focused her attention on listening to the doctor as he told her about the trip she would be making. "It'll be another ten days before she sails, but—"

"Ten days?" Fiona rose and began to pace. "Forgive me, Dr. Killbone, but I expected I would be leaving much sooner."

"I'm sorry," he said, "but that's the best I could do."

At the kind doctor's distraught expression, Fiona forced a smile. "Yes, well, then I will just have to make the best of it, won't I?"

"Are you sure?"

Ten days spent in the same town with Tucker Smith and his fiancée? No, she'd never make the best of that. Never. "Of course," she said.

"Then let me tell you about the trip. It's a mite confusing, but I'll write it all down if you think that'll help."

"Yes, please," she said.

The doctor removed a slip of paper from his pocket and began to draw on it. By the time he finished, Fiona had more questions than tears.

The biggest question of all, the one she dared not ask anyone but the Lord, was about Tucker. She uttered it later that night as she once again lay on the narrow bed, waiting for sleep to overtake her.

"Lord, why did you let me fall in love with him?"

❧

"Lord, why didn't you stop me from loving her?" Tucker scrubbed his face with his hands, then sat back to lean against the hard rocks where he had once toiled happily. "Why didn't you just stop me? Why?"

The words echoed in the small chamber and wrapped around his broken heart. Never would he forget Fiona Rafferty.

Yet his honor forbade him from allowing these feelings free rein. He must keep his word. To do any less would put him in the same category as his father.

That would never happen.

Then there was the situation with Meredith. The poor girl blamed herself for Tucker's mess, and nothing he could say would assuage her guilt.

Never had anything come between them, but the situation with Elizabeth could if not handled properly. He must convince Meredith that she had done nothing wrong, that he bore her no ill will.

But how?

It was a fine mess. Fiona's absence called to his heart while Elizabeth's claims challenged his honor. In a perfect world, the Lord would answer his prayers by telling him to fetch back the one he loved and send the other packing.

God would never instruct anyone to do wrong. Tucker knew better than to consider it.

Still, he tried to cogitate a way around the conundrum. How long Tucker sat in the cave, he had no idea, but when he rose, the cold had stiffened his joints and numbed his legs. Stomping the feeling back into them felt good on more than one level, so he continued it even after it was no longer necessary.

"What in the world are you doing?" Braden called to him from the ridge. "You look like you're doing some kind of crazy dance."

"Come down and try it," Tucker responded. "It's quite therapeutic, actually."

"Is it, now?" He crossed the distance between them to shake Tucker's hand. "I'm a plainspoken man, Tucker," he said, "so I'm going to ask you straight out what's going on here."

"Just stomping around, Braden," he responded.

"No, I mean what's going on with my sister and that city woman over at Ian's place?" He paused. "Amy and I met up with her and Wily a few miles downriver yesterday. I found it odd that a woman would travel all the way from Texas with her pa and not even announce herself with a letter before she arrived."

"Now that you mention it," Tucker said, "that does seem a bit peculiar, doesn't it?"

Tucker's hopes soared. Could he have found a loophole?

"'Course Amy saw it different. She figured it was just a woman's way of surprising her beau. I'm here to ask if you're that woman's beau."

"Her beau?" He thought on it a minute. "I was once. I asked her pa for her hand in marriage."

"And?"

"And he said yes. So did she."

Braden cocked his head to the side. "Are you saying you were dallying with my sister while you had a woman waiting for you back in Texas?"

Before Tucker could respond, Braden hauled off and hit him. Tucker saw stars, then felt the earth spin. Ian stood over him, demanding he stand up again.

"Stop it right now, you two." Ian pushed Braden out of the way and hauled Tucker to his feet. "Fighting is not going to help the situation."

Tucker swiped at his nose, and his hand came away bloody. "I'd stand here and take punches from now until forever if it would bring back Fiona and fix the mess I've made."

"You leave my sister out of this," Braden said.

"I love your sister," Tucker responded. "But Elizabeth is pressing her suit, and I'm not going to break my word."

Ian looked like he wanted to throw his own punch. "I want to hear how this happened, Tucker. How did you lead my sister into believing you were free when you knew you weren't?"

"I didn't know," he said. "I thought we'd agreed that Elizabeth no longer wanted any part of me. Her pa told me she would never bear the Smith name. Said it belonged to a family with no honor."

He practically spat the words, then gave the brothers a look that dared them to comment. When neither responded, he continued.

"I never spoke to Elizabeth directly. I dealt only with her pa, although she stood there and heard every word and never spoke. Under the circumstances, it was the right thing to do, what with Elizabeth being a woman and the flighty sort."

Ian nodded, but Braden barely blinked.

"When Merry and I left Texas, I understood that we did so with no encumbrances except for the ones our father bore. As you both know, I took those on. The Smith name is now clear and free of any hint of dishonor. My intent is to keep it that way."

"So what you're saying," Braden said, "is that you and this woman's da agreed there would be no wedding, only now she's come up here to present herself as your bride?"

"That's the way I see it," Tucker said. "I'm not rightly sure there's another explanation, although it does seem a bit odd that her pa's in Goose Chase, waiting for us."

Ian nodded and rubbed his chin the way he did when he was thinking hard on something. "I reckon we can take the woman at her word. Or. . ."

"Or?" Braden asked.

"Or we can do ourselves a bit of investigating." He gave Tucker a direct look. "What say we all make a trip to Goose Chase together?"

"What do you have in mind?" Tucker asked.

"Just a friendly meeting with your future father-in-law." Ian shrugged. "I have to wonder if he's figuring you've hit it big up here. If so, he might be wanting to change his mind about the value of the Smith name."

Tucker looked at Braden, then back at Ian. "I did use my uncle's money to pay off Pa's debts. I reckon Elizabeth's pa might have heard tell I'd done that and figured I'd sent gold money instead of an inheritance."

"Well, did you tell anyone it was an inheritance?" Braden asked.

"I don't remember," Tucker said. "Probably not. I didn't make much of an explanation to anyone." He squared his shoulders. "Much as I appreciate your offer of help, I'm going to handle this myself."

The Rafferty brothers seemed to be sizing him up. Ian nodded first; then Braden slapped him on the back. "You're a good man, Tucker," he said. "I know you'll do the right thing."

There it was again. *The right thing.* How sick he was of doing *the right thing*.

And he hadn't even come to the hardest part yet.

That came the next day when Tucker reached Goose Chase and walked past the boardinghouse and Doc Killbone's office to step into the lobby of the hotel. He saw Elizabeth's pa from across the room and, for one long minute, tried to decide whether to announce himself or run.

But running was for cowards, and Tucker Smith was no coward. Walking like his boots were making their way through quicksand, Tucker pushed across the Deever House Hotel lobby to stand in front of his father's former business partner.

"Well, now," Cal Bentley said as he rose with difficulty, "I'd know Tucker Smith anywhere." His rheumy gaze studied Tucker a moment. He smiled. "You're doing well up here in the frozen North, I've heard. Quite well, indeed."

"Is that why you're here?" he countered.

The older man looked stunned. Then the mask retuned. "I'm

here because my daughter has decided she can't live without you, Tucker Smith. I'm here to press her case and insist you live up to your promise to marry her."

"Insist?" It was Tucker's turn to do the studying. "Did you anticipate I might reconsider the promise I made?" He took a half step toward the older man. "Were you concerned I might not do the honorable thing, Mr. Bentley?"

"Eh. . .no. . .of course not, son." He fingered the tip of his mustache. "It's just that sending the girl up here without an escort would not have been proper, you see. As her father, it is my duty to see to her welfare until she is safely handed off to her husband." He leaned away from Tucker. "I hope you don't mind, but I found myself with a bit of free time yesterday and wandered up toward the church. I've arranged for the reverend to speak the vows tomorrow morning."

"Tomorrow morning?" As soon as the words were out, Tucker knew he'd shouted them. "Tomorrow morning?" he repeated in a softer voice. "Why so soon?"

Mr. Bentley looked away. "Time is of the essence in these matters. A man can't run his business from all these thousands of miles away, can he?"

"How is the business, Mr. Bentley? Prosperous as ever?"

"Never mind," Elizabeth's father said. "I do just fine. Now what say you and I celebrate the impending nuptials with a juicy caribou steak?"

Food of any kind would have turned his gut, but especially so when Tucker contemplated how he'd be sitting across the table from his father's former business partner, the man who had called in his father's loans and laughed when the elder Smith defaulted and ran.

"Thank you," Tucker said, "but I must decline. Until tomorrow morning," he said as he made his exit. He reached the back of the hotel before he doubled up and lost what little he still had in his stomach.

twelve

"Please stop crying," Fiona said, "or I will never be able to quit."

She looked away from the view of the river out her parlor window to peer at her sisters-in-law through the fog of her tears. Meredith sat on the sofa with her knees beneath her and a feather pillow cradled around her midsection while Amy perched on the edge of a chair.

"Honestly, it's not like I'm falling off the end of the earth. It's just the medical college."

Meredith began to wail again. "But if I'd just kept my matchmaking to myself, you would be here with Tucker and—"

"And Tucker," Amy interjected, "would be marrying for love instead of obligation."

Fiona watched Amy dab at the corners of her eyes with her handkerchief. "Do you really think that's what he's doing, Amy?"

Amy nodded. "Braden thinks so, too."

"Ian's certain of it." Meredith blew her nose most indelicately, then rose to walk to the window. "I'm just so furious at myself, Fiona." She rested her hand on Fiona's shoulder. "Will you ever forgive me? I only meant to. . ." She dissolved into tears.

Fiona gathered Meredith into her arms and patted her back. "Please, dear, don't do this."

A knock at the door silenced Meredith's tears. Amy walked over to open it, then stepped back to reveal Tucker.

"Might I have a moment of Fiona's time?"

Meredith whirled about and blew her nose again. "What do you want to say to her, Tucker?"

"Now, now," he replied. "There are things she must hear

from me before she goes away." He looked beyond Meredith to Fiona. When their gazes met, she felt the collision down to her toes. "You don't have to leave, Fiona. Please reconsider."

Amy squared her shoulders. "Remember, honor is for the Lord to bestow and not for man to decide upon." With that, she took Meredith by the elbow and ushered her out.

Tucker watched the ladies go, seemingly confused at Amy's statement. When he looked at Fiona, she forced herself to avert her gaze.

"Leave the door open, Tucker," Meredith called. "It wouldn't do to compromise Fiona's reputation when she won't be here to defend herself come next month."

"We are just downstairs," Amy added. "And I wager her brothers are nearby. Remember what I said about honor."

All was quiet. Fiona could hear her own breathing. Tucker's, too, she imagined. Then he cleared his throat, and his feet made a shuffling sound on the wooden floor.

"Fiona, look at me." He paused. "Please."

When she complied, her heart sank. Rather than a man whose heart seemed broken, Tucker looked like a fellow about to be wed. He'd had a haircut and a fresh shave, and he wore the dress shirt Meredith had just finished sewing for him last week.

He'd gone to this trouble for Elizabeth, no doubt. Fiona sighed. Oh, how the ugly monster of jealousy was hard to tame.

No matter, for she'd be too busy at the medical college to think about it.

Or him.

"Fiona, you'll never know how hard it was for me to come here today." He caught a ragged breath. "This was supposed to be my wedding day."

"*Was?*" She wrapped her voice around the single word and breathed easier when she'd spoken it aloud.

Tucker inched closer, then seemed to think better of it and, returned to his post by the door frame. "I've been given some time. An answer to prayer, actually."

Her stomach did a flip-flop, and she dabbed at the corners of her eyes. "Oh?"

"The reverend was called away unexpectedly."

"I see." She turned her back on him and steadied herself with a death grip on the windowsill. Outside, the usual activity of the wharf carried on as if it were a normal day in Goose Chase.

"No, Fiona. You don't see."

From the sound of his voice, she could tell he was closer. Her fingers gripped their wooden lifeline that much harder.

"I've. . .that is, we've been given a chance."

She turned toward the sound of his voice and found him nearer than she expected. Backing up as far as she could, Fiona pressed her spine against the sharp angle of the windowsill.

"Yes, I suppose so," she managed to say. "A chance to do the right thing."

Tucker winced at her words, a certain sign he'd come to tell her all the reasons why the two of them were meant to part company.

Fiona searched her mind for something to say that would make him leave. A statement that would cause Tucker Smith to turn and run.

Or maybe to dig in his heels and stay.

She wanted neither. And both.

Then he did the last thing she expected. He didn't run. He didn't dig in his heels.

He kissed her.

&

Tucker waited for Fiona's outrage but hoped for a smile. What he got was stone-cold silence and a face that held no emotion.

Except for her eyes. He thought he glimpsed a spark of hope, perhaps a longing for things to be different.

Then it passed, and she looked away. "Go, Tucker." Her voice was flat as if all the life had gone out of her. "Please, just go."

Tucker threw all caution to the wind and reached for her once more. She sidestepped him, arms crossed around her midsection.

"But, Fiona, it's no use to pretend," he pleaded. "I love you. I always will."

A tear dropped from the fringes of her lashes and traced a path down her cheek to mingle with the strand of hair his embrace had loosened. Tucker knew he would gladly give up all he had to spend his life with Fiona Rafferty.

"Say the word, and I will send Elizabeth packing."

Then came the jab to his conscience. Was this God's plan? Would He suddenly point Tucker away from keeping his word? From doing the right thing and keeping his word to Elizabeth?

Sadly, Tucker knew the answer. Those three words again. *The right thing.*

If only doing the right thing meant having Fiona, as well.

"Tucker?" His name sounded soft as a whisper. Fiona met his stare. "What is God telling you? He wants you to do the right thing, doesn't He?"

He blinked hard. "How did you know?"

"I didn't." Fiona shook her head. "I just know what He's telling me."

Tucker sighed. "And that is?"

She moved toward him, and for a moment, he thought she might fall into his embrace. Instead, she stood up on tiptoe and kissed his cheek.

"Forget me, Tucker," she said as she brushed back the errant strand again. "And I shall attempt to forget you."

"But we're family," he called as she swept past. "How can I forget you? You will always be there at every Rafferty family gathering."

Fiona stopped short and whirled around. "No, Tucker, I won't. But you and Elizabeth will. In time my brothers and their families will come and visit Da. When they do, I'll be there. I ask, however, that you remain absent."

Torment raged inside, and flashes of anger over his predicament made his fists clench. "I won't let you give up your family, Fiona. It's not fair to ask of you."

She shook her head. "You didn't."

"Tucker?" Meredith stood at the end of the hall. "I'm sorry, but Elizabeth is asking for you." She gave Fiona a look that broke Tucker's heart. "I've kept her occupied, but she's threatening to come upstairs. She said you're late for an appointment with her father. Something about him adding you and Elizabeth's children to his will."

Tucker's heart sank at the thought that, as a husband, he would be expected to give Elizabeth children. The reminder, spoken in front of Fiona, seemed too much to consider.

"Thank you, Merry. Tucker and I were just saying good-bye."

Fiona waited until Meredith disappeared back down the stairs before walking purposefully toward Tucker. She stopped close, dangerously close, and Tucker could smell the soft scent of flowers.

Stupid as it was, he inhaled. He was no judge of flowers, but whatever these were, he would always associate them with Fiona. With good-bye.

His heart sank. To his surprise, she reached for his hand and laced her fingers with his.

"I'm letting you go, Tucker, not because I want to, but because I have to."

He was about to protest, about to tell her all the reasons why together they could convince God that their love was good and right. Then she brushed his hand across her cheek, and he felt the dampness of her tears.

She opened her mouth to speak, then seemed to think

better of it. Instead she released her grasp and paused. Once again, their gazes met.

Without caring about the consequences, Tucker enveloped Fiona in an embrace. Slowly, he felt her arms wrap around his shoulders. Then, as his eyes closed, her fists gripped handfuls of his shirt.

Tucker could have gladly stopped time and stood forever with Fiona's curls tickling his chin and her arms holding him tight. Then he felt her sway.

With a sob, she slid from his grasp and disappeared. The slamming of her door felt like a door closing on his heart.

He knew he would never open that part of his heart again, at least not as long as Elizabeth remained his wife. Lifting his damp fingers to his mouth, he tasted the salt of Fiona's tears. It was all he could do not to add his own to them.

&

Tucker stood in the window of his room and watched the harbor until Captain Sven's trawler disappeared from sight. He took a step back and let the lace curtain fall.

He'd chosen this place to stay over the more dignified Deever House Hotel for two reasons. First, he knew his bride-to-be and future father-in-law were staying at the hotel in a corner suite—one he would be expected to share with Elizabeth tonight. More important, Fiona was staying in the room down the hall.

It bordered on pathetic, this need to be close to her despite their conversation to the contrary. Yet Tucker hadn't found the gall to go knock on her door.

She wouldn't answer, he'd reasoned, so ignoring the urge to see her saved him from certain rejection. Besides, Elizabeth adored him; he'd be a fool to chase a dream down the hall when he had reality waiting down the block.

And it was the right thing to do.

Tucker waited until he figured his sister and her family and

Braden and Amy had returned to their rooms at the Deever House, then changed into his new, store-bought church clothes and reached for his hat. He grabbed his Bible instead. Out of habit, he turned to Lamentations and ran his finger down the page until he reached the verse he sought: *"It is of the Lord's mercies that we are not consumed, because his compassions fail not. They are new every morning: great is thy faithfulness. The Lord is my portion, saith my soul; therefore will I hope in him."*

He closed the Bible and said the words again from memory. Now he was ready.

The hotel was two blocks away, and the church stood across the street. The pastor on duty, a fellow by the name of Minter, did the honors while his wife played the wedding march on an old upright piano. Their vows were spoken quickly and sealed with a kiss that fell just shy of the mark.

An hour after the ceremony, Tucker and his new bride saw Elizabeth's father off at the dock. With nothing further to delay the inevitable, Tucker led Elizabeth up the wide staircase to the second-floor corner suite his father-in-law had reserved for them.

The room was as elegant as it was expensive, and the same could be said for his bride. Sensitive to his bride's wedding-night jitters, he excused himself to take a long walk while she made her evening preparations.

Standing at the dock, he stared across the waves to the horizon where the Northern Lights danced in shades of brilliant green. His first thought: *I wish Fiona could see this.*

His second thought: guilt.

Tucker carried that guilt deep in his heart, and no matter how hard he tried, he couldn't cast it off, even when his bride answered the door of their suite with a smile. He knew the source of the smile, and because it was expected of him, he played husband to his wife.

thirteen

The next morning, Tucker awoke to the sound of his new wife depositing last night's dinner into the basin. He held her head until she had nothing left, then brought a wet cloth to wipe her brow.

He repeated the same process three mornings in a row. On the last day of their honeymoon, when Tucker threatened to haul her off to Dr. Killbone, Elizabeth admitted the hotel cooking was not the source of her troubles. Rather, she was three months gone with the child of a cowboy who had been run out of town on a rail by her father. Tucker had been good and truly suckered.

He walked out and stayed gone for two days. When he returned, he half hoped the fellow behind the desk at the hotel would tell him Mrs. Smith had hightailed it out of town in his absence.

Unfortunately, the man handed him the spare key, and when Tucker opened the door, Elizabeth struck up a conversation about the weather as if he'd only gone out for a brief stroll.

Walking past his wife, Tucker stood at the corner window and looked out over the bustling town of Goose Chase. The view of the harbor wasn't as good as the one at the boarding-house, but he could watch the trains roll in and out of the brand-new station down the road.

While Elizabeth reclined on the settee, a wet towel covering the top half of her face, Tucker watched the noon train pull out. He waited until the whistle stopped before turning around and facing his bride.

"I could end this marriage, and no one would blame me."

He clenched his fists. "I've certainly got the law on my side."

Elizabeth peeled off the cloth and gave him a tired look. "You won't do that, Tucker. You're too honorable."

He took a deep breath and let it out slowly. "Why do you think that, Elizabeth?"

His bride struggled to sit upright, allowing the cloth to fall forgotten to the floor. "Because, Tucker Smith, you've enjoyed the marriage bed with me. You'll not leave now. The same moral code that caused you to marry me will keep you from leaving. You're just that kind. You always do the right thing."

She was right, of course.

Tucker brought her home to the little cabin, then quickly agreed the place would never accommodate the two of them. His heart heavier with each passing day, Tucker woke up every morning and put on a smile, even after he acquiesced to his wife's demand that they move into Goose Chase and take up residence in "a proper house."

The house cost as much in gold as the marriage cost in pride, but he endured both with the unfailing hope that the Lord could redeem the situation through the grace He renewed each morning.

Sometime around the fourth week in town, Tucker landed a job with the railroad.

Life became almost good again. Not sweet as it had been in the days with Fiona or before then, when he and Meredith had been making their way as new residents of the frozen state.

Days were no longer filled with empty hours and a wife who paid him no more mind than the barn cats back home or the fellow who delivered the milk. Now Tucker left before daybreak and returned long after Elizabeth had retired for the night. The hours in between were spent chasing the one dream he had left: working on the railroad.

As Elizabeth's belly grew, Tucker played the part of concerned husband. When the day came for her pains to begin, he walked over to Doc's office to inform him, then found Wily and sent word of the impending birth to Meredith.

Meredith needn't have hurried, as Elizabeth labored the rest of that day and through the night. By noon the following day, she'd given up trying and started begging Doc to put her out of her misery.

"There's nothing I can do," Doc explained to Tucker. "I can't hurry something that the Lord's in control of. Besides, the babe's not supposed to come for another month, maybe two, considering you two only married up seven months ago, right?"

Meredith blushed and turned away, but Tucker stood his ground. "That's right, Doc. What are you suggesting?"

Doc Killbone slapped Tucker on the shoulder and shook his head. "You're a good man, Tucker Smith, and I'm not suggesting anything different. What I'm saying is if there's a way to stop this baby from coming, I would have liked to do it."

"There's really nothing you can do?" Meredith asked.

The doctor studied the floor. "There's times when medicine doesn't work. That's when I have to remember that I can still pray." He swung his gaze to meet Meredith's wide-eyed stare. "I suggest you two do the same. That girl in there's not strong like you, Merry Rafferty. I don't know how much longer she can go on. She's lost a lot of blood, and. . .well, frankly, I don't know that she's got much more fight left in her."

A scream sent the doctor running, and a few minutes later, Elizabeth Grace Meredith Smith made her entrance into the world. Meredith fussed over the baby while Doc Killbone saw to Elizabeth.

"Would you like to see the baby?" Meredith hurried over to offer Elizabeth a look at the squalling dark-haired girl.

Elizabeth turned to face the wall. "I can't look at her."

"She's exhausted," Meredith said quickly. "She'll come around when she's stronger."

But she didn't. Three weeks later, when Tucker came home from work, he found a note telling him his daughter was at Doc Killbone's place.

In a panic, Tucker fairly flew down Broadway to the office. The doctor was holding the baby in the crook of his arm and stirring a pot of stew with the other.

"I only stepped out of the examining room for a moment," Doc said as he handed the baby over to Tucker. "When I returned, your wife had disappeared."

"She'll be back." Tucker took the baby home and waited. His daughter's cries brought him back to the doctor's office some hours later. Doc Killbone diagnosed her as being hungry. A substitute was found, and the baby went to live three houses away with the family of a woman who'd only recently lost a child.

Tucker told himself he could get by this way. That he could allow his daughter to grow fat and healthy with a woman who fed her but could not be her mother.

Two days later, he could stand the arrangement no more. Tucker rented out the house on Broadway and went back to his little cabin beside the river. There Meredith helped to feed, diaper, and generally raise the tiny, dark-haired girl she nick-named Lizzie Grace.

Lizzie Grace's size and sickly condition made mention of the early birth unnecessary, and her dark curls and blue eyes made questions of her parentage unwarranted, for she was the spitting image of her mother. Tucker suspected Meredith hadn't been fooled, but he also knew the question would never be asked. He learned that Elizabeth had left Alaska by ship, and letters asking after her sent to his father-in-law went unanswered. Lizzie Grace assumed that her mother had died in childbirth, and no one told her otherwise.

Tucker existed happily for years in the secluded spot, and Lizzie Grace grew into a young girl with coltish long legs and a mane of dark hair that her father had learned to braid with surprising skill. She could run faster than any of her cousins, male or female, and to Tucker's delight took to fishing as if she'd been born to it.

She and Douglas, the closest to her in age and temperament, practically grew up at the river's bank with poles in their hands. When Lizzie Grace wasn't fishing with Douglas, she was following the poor boy around, imitating his every move.

With his sister and her family nearby and his daughter strong and healthy, Tucker would have been content to live out his days watching his daughter grow in the little cabin. One day, however, Meredith came to him with a plea for Lizzie Grace.

"She's a smart girl, Tucker," Meredith said. "She needs to be in a proper school that will prepare her for whatever God's got for her life, and she needs to be going to a real church. Ian and I have been talking about moving to town, and we want you to go with us."

Just like that, Tucker returned to Goose Chase and the house on Broadway that he'd rented out for years. He also went back to the railroad and found the man who had originally hired him now ran the show. He landed a job and went to work the same day.

Ian and Meredith and their three little ones moved in with Tucker and Lizzie Grace, and the house burst at the seams until Ian's house next door was complete. Even though walls and a small stretch of yard separated the families, it was just as common to see a Rafferty child—usually Douglas—in the Smith household as to see Lizzie Grace spending time next door with the Rafferty clan.

Amy and Braden visited often. The pair were happily adding on to the cabin Amy's father had given them and making a life with their children. Their occasional visits to town were met with celebration, and each time, Meredith begged Amy to consider staying for good.

Amy and Braden wouldn't, and Tucker knew it. But he also understood Meredith's need to have female members of the family around her. Occasionally he thought of Elizabeth and wondered where she was; more often his musings landed on the subject of Fiona.

She'd completed her schooling at the medical college with honors and gone to work at a hospital in Seattle. Last time the Rafferty clan got together, Meredith had taken a photograph that Tucker still hadn't found the courage to look at.

Not as long as he was still married to Elizabeth. He couldn't. Instead, he concentrated on doing the right thing and pushing away any hope of a life with Fiona Rafferty.

Seemingly while he watched, his daughter grew and thrived. Meredith proved correct in her estimation that Lizzie Grace needed a proper education and a real church to attend. Under the tutelage of the teachers at Goose Chase School, she proved to possess an intelligence far superior to that of her old dad. And in Sunday school classes, she grew in her love for the Lord, often asking questions Tucker had to go deep into the Bible to answer.

Life was good. Then, three days after Lizzie's thirteenth birthday, a letter arrived. The official document told him that his daughter, Elizabeth Smith, was the sole heir of the Bentley estate, which consisted of three hundred acres that ironically had once been Smith land. The rest, the attorney's letter went on to state, had been spent for back taxes and funeral expenses. Attached to the document were the papers Tucker had signed the week before his wedding.

"Surely he meant this to go to your wife," Ian said after reading the documents.

Tucker sent a letter to the attorney, letting him know that there was another Elizabeth Smith out there somewhere, and some months later, another letter arrived. It included a death certificate and a yellowed clipping from a newspaper in San

Antonio that told the sordid tale of the murder of a Texas belle named Elizabeth Bentley Smith at the hands of a cowboy.

Tucker lit a match and tossed the paper into the fire. The death certificate he placed alongside his marriage documents in the trunk up in the attic.

A weight fell off Tucker's shoulders even as he grieved for the woman Elizabeth had become. He wondered far too often if he could have done something different, if he might have prevented the tragedy and saved Lizzie's mother.

A year went by, then another, and eventually peace returned. Still, something nagged at Tucker. Some not-so-small piece of the puzzle eluded him, and his prayers failed to reveal what that something was.

One day while riding a long stretch of rail, Tucker had a revelation. The missing piece was a red-haired woman who, by now, had surely forgotten the feelings she had for him so long ago.

Right there in the caboose, with snow-covered mountains slipping past and Skagway behind him, Tucker wrote Fiona Rafferty a note on the only paper he could find: a train schedule. Surely true love cared not for the stationery the sentiment was expressed on.

While Tucker did not know Fiona's address, he felt sure Ian or Meredith did. He practiced the words he would say to them, but when he stopped by Ian's home, the words flew away. He handed the letter to his brother-in-law in silence.

Ian looked Tucker in the eye and nodded, then slipped the letter into his pocket.

Months went by and no response came from Fiona, so he wrote again and delivered the letter to Ian to send south. Eventually, Tucker concluded that Fiona wanted no part of him.

Not that he could blame her. That's when he tucked his memories away and promised himself he'd live just fine without them. More important, he wouldn't subject Lizzie Grace to the pain, either.

Some things—and certain people—were better left alone.

So he worked hard at the job he loved, and he made it his life's work to finish raising his beloved daughter and to enjoy his old age with any grandchildren she might one day bring him. The years flew by, and the little girl grew into a quite lively young woman who was as much his daughter as if she were made from the same genes.

Lizzie Grace made him laugh and caused him to shed more than a few tears with her childlike faith in him and in the Lord. From the moment he became her sole parent, Tucker had vowed before God that he would be the kind of papa his own father had not been. It made him proud over the years that, while he hadn't done a perfect job, he'd certainly come close more times than not.

The pain in his heart, however, never completely went away. Whenever a thought of Fiona Rafferty intruded into the present, Tucker stopped what he was doing and said a prayer that the woman God never intended him to be with was safe and happy.

That generally worked to channel his thoughts elsewhere. Once he started praying for exasperating females, he naturally went from Fiona to his daughter.

Lizzie Grace had celebrated her seventeenth birthday by doing two things: declaring that from that day forward she would only answer to the more adult name of Grace, and begging her father for permission to take a part-time job with, of all people, old Doc Killbone.

Tucker agreed to the first and completely refused to allow the second. The last thing he needed was to lose another woman he loved to the medical profession.

fourteen

"It's only six months. After all, the Israelites wandered around on a detour that lasted forty years before the Lord let them settle down. With all the trouble I've been to Him, I should be glad He didn't decide to give me twice the sentence He gave His chosen people."

Dr. Fiona Rafferty continued to mutter under her breath as she guided her motorcar off the boat's wooden ramp and gently around the confusion of stevedores, passengers, and crates, then stopped to consult her notes. Her last glimpse of Goose Chase had been from the deck of a southbound trawler some eighteen years ago, so she'd been careful to include Ian's last letter among her important papers.

The home that she had leased for six months on Ian's recommendation—the one shown on a detailed map she'd tucked into her notebook—was indeed on Third Street, three blocks from the office where she was to report one week from today.

Despite her many misgivings, how wonderful it would be to live near family once again. Some years back, Ian and Meredith had inexplicably moved their growing family to Goose Chase, where Ian went to work for the White Pass and Yukon Railroad. Meredith wrote a long letter attributing their move to better schools and the benefits of being a part of a church community for the first time since she left Texas. Fiona was left to guess whether or not Tucker made the move along with his twin.

"No matter," she whispered. "I'm a grown woman. If I see him—or his wife—it will be fine. We will probably smile, give one another a how-do-you-do, and go our separate ways."

But her words failed to ring true. Knowledge of what she would do would have to wait until the actual moment. In the meantime, she had far too much to consider.

A chill wind ruffled her newly shortened hair and slid inside her collar, making her shiver. While Da had eventually adjusted to his only daughter's decision to become a doctor, her late father probably would have been appalled that she'd lopped off two-thirds of the length of her unruly locks the day after Easter.

Funny how the things she saw as foolish had been so important to Da. Still, the dear man had loved her and the Lord to the very end, only registering the mildest of complaints when she pressed the point of her independence too close to home.

Fiona ran her hand through the abbreviated curls, then set her driving hat atop her head. No matter what Da might have thought, a hairstyle that neither impeded her work nor called undue attention to her womanhood held great merit. At the advanced age of thirty-seven, she'd long since given up the foolishness and frippery of girlhood for a more conservative mode of dress and deportment.

To that end, she would soon have to adjust her wardrobe to Alaska's climate, and fortunately, according to Meredith, a ladies' dress shop stood just around the corner from the office. While Fiona's blue, lightweight wool ensemble was the height of fashion in Seattle, it would soon prove to be the height of foolishness in Goose Chase.

That much about Alaska she did remember—not from experience but from Ian and Braden's tales and from Meredith's letters. When the winter winds blew across the icy terrain, she would be wishing for warmer days—and warmer clothes.

Of all the places she thought God would send her to practice medicine, Alaska was not among them. It was the last place she had expected. Yet God clearly had sent her here, what with the way all the minute details of her move seemed to be orchestrated by what could only be termed a divine hand.

"It's only six months," she reminded herself.

Even with the long-ago promise made to Doc Killbone, she fully believed another doctor would join the old man's practice well before he needed her to move in. Ian's theory was that Doc felt personally responsible for bringing Fiona back to Alaska. Braden, on the other hand, joked that the old man was biding his time until Fiona honed her skills on the unfortunate folks of Seattle.

She smiled at the Lord's unique way of nudging her back to the one place she hadn't quite made her peace with leaving. Fiona shrugged off the thought. "Let it go, old girl."

It was hard to think of either her brothers or Tucker without remembering the idyllic spot where he and the Rafferty men had mined the earth for gold and grown produce twice the size of Oregon's best. But then, it was also hard to think of the man she'd almost given up her dreams for married to another.

Many years had passed, and no doubt Tucker Smith was a happily married fellow who gave no thought to the foolish girl whose heart he'd broken so many years ago. She'd had plenty of opportunities to ask of his welfare or to hear details of his life, but thankfully Meredith had respected her request not to speak of Tucker except in generalities.

Then there were the letters, each destroyed unopened. She hadn't needed to read his apology or suffer his pity. More important, she certainly did not need to be told that their separation was for the best or that his new life was ever so wonderful.

No, best to just let it go. Or rather, to let Tucker Smith go.

And to think she'd actually thought of ignoring her calling

and instead live in the tiny wilderness cabin where Tucker probably still resided. What a fool she'd been. She shook her head as if to dislodge the memory.

Fiona stuffed her notepad back into her bag and squared her shoulders. "It's all for the best, isn't it, Lord? If I'd been fool enough to marry the man, I'd never have gone to medical school."

That settled, Fiona adjusted her hat and placed her gloved fingers on the steering wheel. Despite all her confusion and misgivings over her hasty exit from Alaska some eighteen years ago, she was back, and she'd come to stay—at least for six months.

To celebrate her newfound resolve, Fiona picked up her speed. The sooner she found her home on Third Street, the sooner her new life, albeit a temporary one, would begin.

In keeping with safe driving procedures, Fiona drove right down the center of Broadway, veering only slightly to the right or left to dodge the plentiful and disgusting road apples that were a natural hazard of last century's horse-drawn carriages.

Although she avoided those hazards as she motored along, she couldn't miss their scent. "All the more reason to replace such an outdated conveyance with an automobile," she said as she wrinkled her nose. "For transportation there is no finer—"

An impediment of the human variety came charging into her path, and she turned hard to the right just in time to nearly graze him. She might have stopped and given the oaf a lecture in proper pedestrian deportment had the fellow not raised his fist and, in a loud voice, called into question her driving skills.

Rather than waste words on the ruffian, she pushed the Ford to its limit and left him standing in her wake. Like as not, this would be the last she'd see of him anyway. Men of that ilk generally did not frequent places where decent folk were seen.

❧

Tucker chewed on the dust in his mouth and pondered his near miss with eternity. While he loved Jesus with everything in him, he'd never thought when he sipped his first cup of coffee this morning that he might be headed for heaven this afternoon. Besides, he'd always expected the Lord would call him home during one of his fits of apoplexy over Lizzie Grace's latest stunt.

Or as she preferred to be called: Grace.

He set his hands on his hips and stared down the back end of the offending automobile. *Of all the nerve.*

The woman at the wheel hadn't even stopped. And why in the world was she driving down the middle of the road? Even a tried-and-true horseman like himself knew to veer to the right or the left depending on which direction he traveled.

He gave the contraption one last look, then swiped at the road dust with his hat and set it back atop his head. In all his born days, he'd never seen a horseless carriage with a driver that dangerous. Back in Texas, he'd ridden bulls that followed a straighter path.

"Goes to show you the horse can never be replaced, especially not by one of those death traps." Tucker watched the motorcar head left onto Third Street, then disappear. "Her husband ought to be shot for allowing such a menace out of the house."

"Well now, that's a fine way for a man to talk."

Tucker turned at the sound of Meredith's voice. "Did you see what she did? Why, the woman practically aimed at me."

"Aimed at you?" Meredith affected that I-don't-believe-you look he knew so well. "From what I saw, you were standing in the middle of the street."

"I wasn't standing; I was walking. And for your information, that contraption was driving in the middle of the street. What person in his—or should I say *her*—right mind would drive down the middle of the road?"

Meredith turned up her pretty nose and shook her head. "The sort of person," she said in a voice that held far too much amusement to be taken seriously, "who is looking to avoid a collision with animals or persons who might be too near the edge of the sidewalk."

"That's exactly the type of answer I would expect from someone with no driving skills." Tucker stepped aside to let a horse and buggy pass, then regarded his sister through narrowed eyes. "I can see now why Ian refuses to allow you to learn."

To Tucker's horror, his twin's eyes welled with quick tears, and she hurried away. He stood transfixed. "I've done it well and good this time."

Mrs. Simpson, wife of the mayor, gave him a look that confirmed his statement as she swept past. "Seems to me a man ought to stay to the sidewalk and hold his tongue unless he's got something nice to say."

"What? Well, for the love of—" Tucker opened his mouth but couldn't get it to cooperate. Finally, he shrugged and ducked his head.

He caught up with his sister on the sidewalk outside Doc Killbone's office. "Come on, Merry. You know I didn't mean it."

"I know a man often says things he means only to discover he shouldn't have."

She shrugged, and Tucker's heart sank. The only thing worse than arguing with Meredith was to watch her give in so easily.

"No, here's the truth. I'm a first-class fool." Tucker gathered his sister into his arms and kissed the top of her head. "Forgive me, please."

Meredith stepped out of his embrace, her eyes glistening. "No, you're right. I'm not fit to drive an automobile."

Tucker crossed his arms over his chest. "Who in the world would want to? One of these days, somebody's going to pass a law against them. I just know it." He caught the beginnings of a smile on his sister's face. "Now that's better. So, tell me. What brings you to town today?"

A strange look came over her, quickly followed by a shrug. "I'm meeting an old friend," she said.

For the first time, Tucker noticed the basket she carried. "What's this?" he asked as he lifted the cloth to spy its contents. "Preserves and fresh-baked bread? And is that a pie? Maybe I'll come along with you to meet that old friend." He took a step back. "Say, what old friend are you talking about? Surely not someone from Texas."

She shook her head. The slightest smile touched her lips, then quickly disappeared.

"Merry, you're not going to tell me, are you?"

His twin gave Tucker a direct look, then giggled. "If you want to know, you'll just have to follow me."

"Maybe I will," he said as he fell into step beside her. "Say, what's this friend's name?" When Meredith ignored the question, Tucker tried again. "At least tell me whether this is a he or a she."

Meredith stopped in the middle of the sidewalk and set the basket beside her. Hands on her hips, she stood up on tiptoe to come slightly closer to looking him in the eye.

"Tucker Smith, do you honestly think I would be taking a welcome basket to a *he*? What kind of woman do you think I am? Why, I've never even looked at another man since Ian Rafferty came along."

Tucker hung his head. This was not a discussion he would ever win. Time for him to make a good retreat.

❧

As she watched her brother head back up the street, Meredith knew her irritation at him was due more to her conversation with her husband that morning than with anything Tucker might have said. Still, she couldn't tell him that, nor could she tell him of Fiona's return to Goose Chase.

She'd tried many times over the past month, to no avail. The promise Fiona held her to way back in 1899 still tied Meredith to a time that she hated to be a part of. In her haste to see her brother happy, she'd done the one thing that assured he never would find what he sought.

Now, with her prayers answered and Fiona back in Goose Chase, she had no idea how to tell the two of them they were meant to be together. It was silly, this need to make up for the horrible wrong she'd done to them by her letter to Elizabeth all those years ago.

Some days she thought she'd been used of the devil by sending that letter. Then she watched Tucker's daughter, Lizzie Grace, and knew the girl was meant to be in Tucker's world.

Of course, the why and how of that was also a discussion she and Tucker had never had. There was no need. Elizabeth Grace Meredith Smith was as much a part of Meredith's family as were her own children.

The thought of her children brought Meredith to her eldest, Douglas, and the tiff his newest cause had brought on between her and Ian. In nearly twenty years of marriage, she'd only fought with her husband on a handful of occasions, none of which held enough significance for her to be able to remember the details the next day.

This time, however, was different. The son she loved wanted to go to war to make the world safe. What parent would not be proud of a young man willing to give up his life for a cause greater than his own?

Meredith dabbed at her eyes with her handkerchief and hurried up the block to where the motorcar sat. What parent would willingly give up a son? As soon as the thought occurred, she sighed. If her heavenly Father could willingly send His Son, she had no excuse.

Still, did Douglas have to leave Alaska to serve his country?

The registration for the draft next month only involved men twenty-one years old and older. Douglas was just eighteen. Why couldn't he wait until he was older? Perhaps there was another way.

Without Ian to support her, she had considered going to Tucker for help—until he proved just how exasperating he could be on occasion. Then there was the situation with Fiona's return.

"Is this person a man or a woman, indeed?"

Then, right there on the sidewalk in front of 233 Third Street, the Lord delivered the most brilliant plan to her. At least she hoped it was the Lord, because she would definitely need His help to pull it off.

Meredith smiled. She'd also need Lizzie Grace, but the dear girl would never have to know.

fifteen

Fiona heard the muttering before she heard the knock. She'd been halfway between the kitchen and the small room where she planned to set up her bed when Meredith's voice floated in through the open window.

"Of all the nerve. Thinking I was paying a visit to a he. Why in the world would he even think something like that? As long as I live, I'll never understand why the Lord saw fit to make me twin to a man who—"

Fiona opened the door, ending Meredith's monologue. The basket nearly pitched forward as Meredith enveloped Fiona in an embrace.

"I've missed you terribly." Meredith set the basket down and held Fiona at arm's length. "I know Ian and I saw you three years ago last summer, but it seems like forever." Her eyes went wide. "Fiona Rafferty, you've cut off all your hair."

"Well, not all of it." She patted her shoulder-length bob. "Just the part that got in the way."

Meredith made a complete circle around Fiona, then shook her head. "What's it like? Do you miss it?"

"Miss the mess? Of course not." Fiona reached for the handle of the basket and ushered her sister-in-law inside. "Come get out of this wind. It's going to blow you away."

"Oh, Fiona, that's the hazard of living in Goose Chase. I'm used to it."

Fiona shut the door and carried the basket into the kitchen. As Meredith swept in and began to unload the contents of the basket, Fiona settled at the table and watched her work.

"I'm wondering something, Merry," she said after a moment.

She paused to turn and face Fiona. "What's that?"

"Why did my brother bring you here?" Fiona paused. "The real reason."

Meredith paused before saying, "Fiona, you know I've always respected your request not to speak of Tucker in my letters or on those rare times when we've been together." She lifted her gaze to meet Fiona's. "So, if I were to answer that question, it might tell you more than you want to know."

Fiona opened her mouth to speak, then thought better of it. Perhaps Meredith was right. Details of Tucker Smith's life were best left to his wife.

"All right, then," Fiona said. "Why don't I make some coffee? You can catch me up on all the wonderful things my brilliant niece and nephews are doing."

"Brilliant?" Meredith chuckled. "Brilliant at driving their poor mother to distraction." She sobered a moment. "Seriously, they are wonderful children. A mother couldn't be prouder."

Fiona reached for the pail of water she'd drawn only moments before Meredith's arrival and poured just enough in the pot for four cups of coffee. After lighting the stove, she set the pot atop the burner and returned to her place at the table. In her absence, Meredith's face had taken on a worried look.

"Something's wrong. What is it, Merry?"

Her sister-in-law reached for Fiona's hands and held them tight. "It's Douglas." She paused to study the pattern on the tablecloth before looking up. "He wants to join the war effort."

"Why, that's wonderful, Merry," Fiona said. Behind her, the water began to gurgle in the pot. "We all need to do our part for the boys serving our country. What is it he wants to do?"

Tears welled in Meredith's eyes. "He wants to join the army, Fiona. My boy wants to fight for his country."

"Fight?" The word caught in Fiona's throat. To her mind, Douglas would always be the red-haired infant she'd cuddled eighteen years ago. He would be grown now, a man to most of the world.

Back in Seattle, she'd lost a neighbor to the campaign against the Kaiser, and in her practice, she'd seen far too many of the walking wounded who'd been sent home.

"Yes," Meredith said softly.

Fiona squeezed Meredith's hands. "Well, surely Ian will talk sense into the boy."

The first fat tear landed on the oilcloth, followed in quick succession by several more. Meredith's lip trembled as she cleared her throat.

"That's the worst part. Ian's supporting him in this."

"Surely not," Fiona said. "Why, Douglas is still a lad. Why in heaven's name would anyone suggest he'd be fit for fighting?"

Meredith shook her head. "He's nearly nineteen. By the time I was his age, I had already. . ."

She didn't have to complete the thought. Fiona knew of Meredith's trek from Texas to Alaska, although she'd only been privy to the vaguest details as to why. Something about a bit of trouble Meredith's pa had encountered—trouble Tucker had remedied with an inheritance from their uncle Darian.

Fiona forced her mind back to the issue at hand. "What's the cause of this, Merry? Has my brother encouraged Douglas's patriotism?"

"Yes," a male voice sounded from outside.

Her attention shot to the open window where Ian Rafferty stood. "A little birdie told me there was pie and fresh coffee to be had here."

Bolting to the door, Fiona met her brother halfway. He greeted her with a hug, then twirled her around and set her back down. Reeling, she smoothed her hair back into place.

"Mercy, girl, where's the rest of you?" Ian towered over her, a mock scowl decorating his features. "You've gone and cut off your curls."

"Oh, bother, Ian, get on inside and let's talk about something more important than the length of my hair."

"I like it, actually," Meredith said. "It's much prettier than a plain old braid."

"Never mind, Merry." Ian stomped his boots until satisfied he'd removed most of the mud, then strode inside. "I find your braid to be anything but plain. And I have similar feelings about the rest of you, darling wife."

Fiona watched him kiss the top of his wife's head, then felt an unfamiliar wistful tug. As soon as the feeling came, she pressed it away. Years of training her mind had caused her to perform the action almost without thought.

What good did wishing and hoping do?

"So, do you like the little place we picked out, Fiona, dear?" Ian removed the coffeepot from the stove. "Merry would have preferred something nearer our place, but I told her you'd like being close to your office."

While Meredith engaged Ian in a discussion of the merits of living on the east side of town as opposed to the west, Fiona found three mugs in the second cabinet she opened. Filling two, she slid them before her brother and sister-in-law, then reached back to pour hers.

The banter continued for another few minutes before Ian cleared his throat and regarded Fiona with a sideways look. "So, that your Tin Lizzie at the curb?"

"Tin Lizzie?" Fiona chuckled. "Well, if you're referring to my 1916 Ford, then yes, that's mine. Do you like it?"

Ian pretended to think for a moment. "I reckon it's fine for a city girl, but let's see how it fares through an Alaskan winter."

"I'm more worried about how *I'll* fare through an Alaskan winter," Fiona said. "I've heard here on the peninsula the weather's comparable to Seattle. Is that true?"

"Actually last winter when you all were posting snowfall records, we fared pretty well," Ian said. "But then, I'm sure my wife will be glad to help you shop for anything you might need to keep warm."

Meredith nudged her husband. "Very funny." She turned her attention to Fiona, placing her hands atop Fiona's. "I'm so glad you're here."

"Thank you." She winked at Ian. "I'm glad I'm here, too. It's not what I thought I'd be doing, but I'm sure it didn't take the Lord by surprise."

"Speaking of surprise," Meredith said, "the whole town is wondering why Doc Killbone suddenly decided to retire. He's not saying a word, but I wondered if maybe you knew."

"Now, Merry," Ian warned. "It's really none of our business." He paused. "Unless the doctor's in ill health. In that case, I would want to bring his situation before the church elders since he's got no family up here."

"No," Fiona said. "He only mentioned that he was ready to pass on his patients to someone younger and that he'd like me to stay on while a proper search is conducted." She shrugged. "I assumed he was ready to retire. Speaking of the doctor, he said he would leave a key with you, Merry."

She shook her head. "Plans changed. He's still in Goose Chase. I guess he figured even a week without a doctor was too long for our bustling city."

Fiona laughed. "Now that's the Doc Killbone I remember. I suppose I should find my way down there this week and visit with him before he goes."

Meredith nodded. "Yes, but wait until tomorrow. I have the most wonderful idea. Why don't you join us tonight for dinner? It's not caribou, I promise."

A positive response lay on the tip of her tongue, but then Fiona thought better of it. She'd most likely see Tucker Smith eventually. It was highly unlikely he would go long periods of time without seeing his twin. Still, she'd traveled a long way to return to a place where bad memories abounded. Perhaps a good night's sleep would better prepare her for whatever situations entering Ian and Meredith's home would bring.

Thankfully, Ian saved her from having to decide. "Not tonight, dear. I've got a meeting of the church elders, and I'm sure Fiona is exhausted."

"Indeed, I am a bit tired." She glanced out the window to see a tall, red-haired fellow driving a wagon, a dark-haired girl at his side. As he halted to swing off the seat, Fiona knew the fellow was Douglas.

She met him at the curb and wrapped her arms around him. "When did you grow to twice my height, Douglas?" She leaned past him to smile at the young lady in the wagon. "I'm Fiona, Douglas's aunt."

The girl held tight to the reins with one hand and shook Fiona's hand with the other. "Pleased to meet you, Miss Rafferty. I'm Grace."

"That's *Dr.* Rafferty, know-it-all," Douglas said. "Now make yourself useful and fetch something out of the box."

"Stay right where you are, Lizzie Grace." Ian strode toward them, and for a moment, Fiona was struck by the similarity of father and son. She might as well have been looking at the same person in two generations. Funny, but had it really been so many years since Ian was Douglas's age? Some days it felt like yesterday.

"Something wrong, Aunt Fiona?" Douglas asked.

"No, darling," she said. "I was just thinking back to when your father was young and strong like you."

"Hey now," Ian called from the back of the wagon, "don't call me an old man yet. I may be the older of the two, but I guarantee I'm the stronger. Let's just see who gets more of these trunks inside than the other."

At Ian's challenge, Douglas picked up his pace. Grace chuckled. "It's always like this. You should see them when it comes to chopping wood. Between those two and my father, the whole town of Goose Chase could stay warm from what they chop."

Fiona drew near the wagon. Something about the young woman seemed so familiar. The eyes, she'd seen them somewhere before. But where?

"Stand back, Dr. Rafferty. Here they come again," Grace called as the door opened and two burly redheads poured out.

While the men and their cargo went in the front door, Meredith came strolling out the back. "Hello, Liz—" She paused to shake her head. "Sorry, it's going to take some time for me to get used to this. Let me start over. Hello, Grace. I see you've met Dr. Rafferty."

When the girl nodded, Meredith continued. "Fiona, Grace reminds me of you when you were her age. We're trying to get her father to understand that perhaps God has plans for Grace that include using her gifts as a healer."

"He's so old-fashioned," Grace said as she rolled her eyes. "He was furious when I told him I was thinking about becoming a nurse so I could join the war effort. Can you believe it?"

"Now, dear," Meredith said, "this is the first I've heard of your interest in such a thing."

The girl edged closer to the side of the wagon. "My friend Helen from church just left to study at Grace Hospital in Toronto. She's got her heart set on joining the Canadian Expeditionary Forces. They go all over the world, you know?"

Fiona noticed Meredith's face had gone white, so she carefully steered the girl away from such dangerous waters. "Why nursing, Grace? Have you ever thought of becoming a doctor? It takes a bit longer and you'd most likely miss active-duty status in this war, but you'd be helping a whole lot of people back here." She paused. "A great many of our fighting men have returned and are in need of follow-up care by trained doctors. Perhaps you'd like to know what medical school entails."

"Oh, yes, do tell."

The girl hung on each word, and by the time Fiona offered to continue the discussion at the office sometime in the near future, Douglas was climbing back onto the buckboard, and Ian looked as if he might be in need of a nap. Meredith mouthed a discreet "Thank you" as Ian came to stand at her side.

"Thank you for bringing the rest of my things," Fiona said. "I could never have managed to get them all inside without you Rafferty men." She turned to Grace. "And it was lovely meeting you, dear. Do come and see me down at the office soon."

"I will," Grace said. "I promise." She offered Fiona a troubled look. "But do we have to tell my papa? He's awful cantankerous when it comes to this subject."

"I think you shouldn't be dishonest with your father," Ian said. "He's a good man and only wants the best for you. If he forbids you to do something, you mustn't do it."

"And while you're contemplating my father's wise words," Douglas interjected, "hand over the reins. I don't ride in a wagon with a woman driving."

Grace objected to the statement and the demand, and soon the pair was embroiled in a war of words. Meanwhile, Ian gave Fiona a kiss on the cheek and headed for the back of the empty wagon.

"Climb in, wife," an exhausted Ian said to Meredith. "I don't believe I'll be walking home today."

"Dear, this happens every time you try to keep pace with Douglas." She allowed her husband to hand her up into the wagon. "Perhaps you should take on our younger son and let the elder one be."

Ian chuckled and gestured to the front of the wagon where Douglas had reluctantly given up on seizing the reins from Grace. "I think our elder son has met his match."

Meredith settled her skirts demurely around her, then smiled at her husband. "Happens every time a Rafferty takes on a—"

"Off with you now," Ian quickly called to Grace. "I'm hankering for a soft chair and a bowl of stew before my meeting at church."

The dark-haired girl set the horses moving, then looked over her shoulder at Ian. "Will Papa be at that meeting?"

Ian's answer was lost in the clatter of horses' hooves, and soon Fiona stood alone in the silence. "Well, Lord," she said as she trudged toward the door and the mountain of boxes that begged to be unpacked, "I don't know for sure what Your plan is, but then, when did that ever stop me from following anyway?"

sixteen

Fiona's penchant for neatness kept her up half the night, thus she'd slept well past dawn. Or at least past the time dawn would have broken in Seattle.

Thus her breakfast had become a midmorning snack, and her early morning visit with Doc Killbone had been postponed until after lunch. She found plenty to busy herself with, however, starting with putting away the last of her personal effects.

Only one trunk had remained unpacked last night, and she opened it now. She quickly hung the clothing it contained in the armoire, then removed the paper separating the clothing from her weakness: an extensive collection of shoes. There atop the matched rows of footwear purchased at the likes of Nordstrom's and the Bon Marche sat a hideous pair of eighteen-year-old sealskin boots.

She lifted one out and gingerly examined it. Considering its age and the heavy use it had taken during that one memorable Alaskan summer, the boot had held together remarkably well.

"How many times have I tried to give these away?" Fiona sighed. "More times than I could count. Come winter, I might be glad I saved them."

Fiona removed its mate and set the pair together in the back of the armoire, then began arranging the other shoes around them until the trunk was empty. With the last trunk set on the back porch for Douglas to retrieve that evening, Fiona ran out of busywork. Only her visit to the clinic remained undone.

Forgoing a lunch that likely wouldn't settle well on her nervous stomach, Fiona decided to drive, then at the last minute chose to walk the short distance. She bypassed Doc

Killbone's office to browse through the offerings at the Goose Chase Mercantile. While it would in no way be mistaken for Nordstrom's, the mercantile did give the local Sears and Roebuck some serious competition.

She'd walked through departments containing outerwear, underwear, and footwear, when she came to the section reserved for the extreme cold of the Alaskan winter. Not surprisingly, it was the largest department.

A bald-headed fellow in clothing that looked as if it came off the racks from that very department called to her as he emerged from the back of the store. "Need anything, you let me know, miss."

"Thank you," she responded. "I'll do that."

But she wasn't shopping, just looking. It was something to do to pass the time until she collected her wits and retraced the steps of her past to the front door of the medical clinic.

Fiona had almost decided she was ready when she stumbled upon a shelf containing sealskin boots. Front and center were a pair of boots identical to the ones hiding in the back of her closet.

She ran her hand over the soft fur and closed her eyes. The smell of fresh air and freshly cleaned fish assaulted her nose and made her smile. Sunday afternoons at the river rolled past in quick succession.

When the action stopped on the day she first saw Elizabeth's face, she opened her eyes. To her shock, there stood Elizabeth herself. Her heart jumped into her throat, and Fiona gasped.

"I'm sorry, Dr. Rafferty. I didn't mean to frighten you."

The young woman from yesterday leaned against a pile of blankets, not some ghost from eighteen years past. Fiona shook her head and let out a long breath.

"How are you, Grace?" Fiona glanced up at the Regulator clock situated over the handguns-and-ammunition counter. "Shouldn't you be at school?"

"I am furthering my education," she said a bit too defensively. "I came to see if you're willing to take me on as a student."

Fiona took the girl's elbow and led her away from the memories. "Whatever are you talking about?" she asked when they stepped out into the sunshine.

"Douglas said he heard tell your papa wanted to marry you off, too." Blue eyes stared down from a superior height and begged honesty of Fiona.

"That's true," she said, "and I assume my nephew heard this from his father." When Grace shrugged, Fiona continued. "My father thought I would have a much easier life should I choose to find a husband and bring babies into the world." Strangers were beginning to take notice of Fiona, so she linked arms with Grace and set out walking.

"That's funny," Grace said. "You do bring babies into the world. Many more than if you'd had them yourself."

"Yes, I do." Fiona chose her words carefully. "But if I was to be completely honest, my father was right. To have chosen marriage and a family, well, that would definitely have been the easier life." She paused to let the girl think about her words, then pressed on. "How old are you, Grace?"

"Seventeen," she said.

"When will you be eighteen?"

Grace smiled. "Eleven months and two days."

They walked along in silence until Grace stopped short. "I don't know which I want, to tell you the truth. I wonder if you might help me decide."

Fiona shook her head. "Whatever do you mean?"

"Simple." She offered Fiona a broad smile, and the absurd feeling of familiarity returned. "I'm not asking for a job, because that would be defying my papa, which would be wrong."

"Yes, it would."

"But if you were to let me come over to the clinic sometimes, just to watch you and see what you do. . ." She paused. "Well, I mean if I'm not working and you're not paying me, then it can't be a job, right?"

Thankfully, Doc Killbone saved Fiona from having to respond. He stepped out onto his porch and called to her. "I wondered when you two would stop circling."

Fiona embraced the doctor, older now but no less spry. He peered at Grace over the tops of his spectacles. "Well, now, isn't this interesting? Shouldn't you be in school, Lizzie Grace?"

"I got out early today," she said. "Finished up at lunch."

"Does your teacher know that?"

Grace squared her shoulders and affected a serious look. "I'm almost done with school, Dr. Killbone. If I didn't feel so bad that Douglas is still working on his studies, I would've already completed mine."

"She's a good girl," the doctor said. "Always looking out for her—"

"Fiona Rafferty, is that you?"

Fiona whirled around to see an older woman crossing the street toward her. "Yes, I'm Fiona Rafferty. Do I know you?"

"Afternoon, Miz Minter," Doc Killbone said. "Pleasure to see you this afternoon. How's the reverend?"

"Strong, fit, and ready to dance a jig, thanks to your good care," she said.

"Now, now. No dancing for another month or so. Seriously, though, is he staying off that leg?"

Mrs. Minter nodded. "The elders met last night to divide up his duties so that he can follow your orders."

She touched a blue-veined hand to the old doctor's sleeve. "He and I are in your debt."

"You pay that debt every time you say a prayer for me. I am willing to guess it's me who owes you and the reverend by now."

She smiled. "Whatever will we do when you leave?"

Doc Killbone smiled. "Well, now, I'm glad you asked. Meet my temporary replacement, Fiona Rafferty."

"*Dr.* Fiona Rafferty," Grace said.

"Dr. Rafferty," the woman echoed. "Oh, my, then it's true." Her eyes misted. "I thought I'd never see you again to tell you how sorry I am. And now it's twice as sweet because I can congratulate you on making your dream come true."

"Sorry?" She looked from Doc Killbone back to Mrs. Minter. "Do we know one another?"

"Seattle to Skagway, 1899," she said. "Although I actually met you over corn bread at your daddy's table in Oregon."

"The preacher's wife." Fiona shook her head. "Oh, my, I was awful to you. Just awful." She reached for the older woman's hand. "Will you ever forgive me?"

"No, dear, it's I who must ask for your forgiveness. Yes, you were young." She chuckled. "And you were quite brash, if I might be so bold to say."

Fiona flushed and ducked her head. Her cheeks burned with shame at the remembrance of things she'd said to this poor woman.

"No, don't be ashamed, dear," the pastor's wife said. "In truth, your words have chased me for some years. At first I was mad. Really mad."

"For good reason," Fiona said. "I should never have—"

"Oh, no, dear, don't you see? You asked an important question, one that I had to search long and hard to answer." She smiled at the doctor, then squeezed Fiona's hand. "Do you remember asking that question?"

Fiona nodded and met Grace's questioning gaze. "I'm ashamed to say that I asked this dear lady what she did. I treated her horribly. If I remember correctly, I made you cry."

"Oh, no, Fiona. No." Mrs. Minter shook her head. "I'd say we were even. How did you like the accommodations I arranged for your first trip to Goose Chase?" She looked over at the doctor. "I sent her here on my uncle Boris's trawler, and I made sure she didn't sail out until he had a boatload of the nasty stuff."

Fiona giggled. "I still remember the smell of that fish."

The quartet shared a laugh. Then Mrs. Minter reached for Grace's hand. "You're the future, Lizzie Grace. Be bold like Fiona here. Don't be afraid to ask, 'What do I do?' To think she's a doctor now."

"Yes, well, that's a pretty speech, Miz Minter, but if you will excuse us, I'm going to steal Fiona away so we can go over some details before I turn this clinic over to her."

"Come, Lizzie Grace," Mrs. Minter said, "I'll walk you back to school."

"Oh, that's not necessary."

Mrs. Minter released her grasp on Fiona and latched on to Grace. "Oh, I think it is. Of course, I could just walk you home. Is your father there, dear?"

Doc Killbone chuckled as he watched the pair walk away. "Did you really ask her that?"

Fiona ducked her head. "I'm afraid so."

The doctor looked as if he were about to comment, then thought better of it. "Shall we go inside? I'm anxious to talk to you about all those years we've been apart."

"Now, now," she said as she stepped inside, "I did write."

He chuckled as the door closed behind them. "Yes, you did, and this old man saved every letter. Now, what say I put on a pot of fresh coffee while we go over clinic procedures?"

"Coffee?" Fiona smiled. "Doc, you read my mind."

"No, I didn't. Your brother told me that the way to your heart was through your coffee cup. I know we said you would start next week, but I'm itching to leave, so I was hoping you'd take one sip of my coffee and agree to start tomorrow." He paused. "I'm hoping I can get you to agree to a year of work here instead of six months."

"Doc," Fiona said slowly as she caught the first wonderful whiff of coffee brewing, "that had better be some exceptional coffee, because my present obligation is to return to teaching at the university at the end of my six months here."

The doctor smiled. "Well, let's just see, shall we?"

seventeen

Tucker paced the parlor, a note from Rev. Minter's wife crumpled in his hand. So Lizzie Grace had skipped out on school again. He'd received a similar note just last week when the preacher's wife had notified him of a conversation she'd had with Lizzie Grace outside the Goose Chase clinic.

Was she just passing by, or was Lizzie Grace at the clinic to beg Doc Killbone for a job as his nurse again? Either way, she'd disobeyed. It wouldn't do to let her get away with such behavior, but short of packing her off to boarding school, what could he do?

She was as strong willed as. . . He paused to think the statement through and realized he could blame her temperament on no one but himself.

Meredith assured him on a regular basis that his daughter was perfectly normal and well behaved for everyone but her father. At church, she was the model of propriety and an example to the younger ones, while at school, she excelled despite the fact that, because she had entered school late, she was a full year older than any of the other students except Douglas.

No, the problem of her discipline lay in the fact that his daughter knew she had him twisted around her pretty pinky finger. Hard as he tried, he had not yet figured out how to wriggle out of her grasp.

The back door opened and closed, and Tucker squared his shoulders. "Elizabeth Grace, come here, please."

To his surprise, Meredith was the one who stepped into the parlor. "I'm sorry," she said. "I know it's late, but I'm afraid we sat too long over cake and coffee. Grace is helping with the dishes.

She'll be along shortly." Meredith touched his arm. "Change of subject. You should have been there tonight. You can't keep avoiding Fiona forever."

"I'm not avoiding her." He crushed the paper in his fist. "Neither am I seeking her. I haven't yet seen her because my job keeps me away for long periods, and you know I've been working that new stretch of track up north." He waved away anything she might have said to the contrary. "Currently my issue is with my daughter. She's missing school again."

"Oh, pshaw, Tucker. That girl could teach at that school. Don't think I don't realize the only reason she still puts up with going is because she wants to see Douglas finish. Another month, and they'll be issuing diplomas anyway. Once she gets that, you'll have a whole other set of worries, but right now, the girl is fine. A little bored, maybe, but fine."

Tucker tried to argue but could find no cause. Rather, he sank into the nearest chair and massaged the bridge of his nose to stave away the dull throbbing that once again threatened.

"Are you having another headache?" Meredith knelt beside the chair. "That's the third one this week."

Truthfully, he'd had one almost without fail every day for the last three weeks, maybe longer. The headaches plagued him mostly in the evening, but on occasion they hit him in the late afternoon, which interfered with his ability to work. Oddly, he never woke up with one.

"I insist you see the doctor about this," Meredith said.

He looked down at his twin and smiled. The effort made him wince.

Meredith climbed to her feet and planted her hands on her hips. "That's it, Tucker Smith. I'm making an appointment for you at the clinic. And before you argue with me, I will remind you that I happen to know that because you've been gone the better part of the last month, you have four days off starting tomorrow." She paused, eyes narrowed. "And if you don't go,

I may be forced to use blackmail."

"Blackmail?"

"Yes." Her smile broadened. "I am your twin sister, Tucker Smith, which means I have been party to almost every misdeed you've performed since leaving the cradle. Would you really like any of those stories told to your daughter?"

Tucker furrowed his brow. "I don't know what you're talking about. I was the model of propriety as a lad. Why, the whole town knew what a good fellow I was. I guess you're forgetting about the annual citizenship awards I received."

Meredith shook her head. "I guess you're forgetting about the lye soap-and-honey incident at the church quilting bee. Then there was the suspicious fire at Mr. Jenson's outhouse." She snapped her fingers. "Oh, and there was the time that you and Buzz Landry took the clothes off Widow Cooper's clothesline and strung them up all over—"

He rose and held his hands up, then blinked hard to push back the jab between his brows. "All right. You've made your point. I'll go see Doc Killbone tomorrow."

She gave him a suspicious look. "What time?"

"Never mind, Merry."

His sister stood staring, arms crossed over her chest. "I'm reminded of the time the reverend found the pages of his Bible glued together. Then there was the shaved cat incident over at—"

"First thing." He met her gaze. "I mean it."

❧

Fiona's first day of work started out with a disaster. The dress she'd carefully chosen and ironed lost a button as she was slipping it on. Choosing a summer frock sprigged in roses, Fiona made it all the way through her morning routine only to spill half a bowl of oatmeal down the front of it while trying to juggle her bowl and her coffee cup. While she took solace in the fact it wasn't coffee she wore on her trek back upstairs to change, she had lost valuable time.

Thankfully, she arrived to find no line formed outside the clinic doors. Stepping inside, she instantly smelled fresh coffee brewing.

"Doc," she called as she removed her hat and set her handbag aside. "I'm sorry I'm late. You wouldn't believe the trouble I had just getting out the door. Say," she said as she followed the luscious scent to the kitchen in the back of the building. "I thought you were leaving yesterday."

She pushed back the curtain separating the kitchen from the adjacent hallway and stepped into a room that held the combined scents of fresh coffee and baked bread. At the cook-stove stood Grace.

"What are you doing here?" Fiona suppressed a smile. Obviously the girl's papa hadn't been consulted, nor had her schooling been considered.

To her credit, Grace looked reasonably contrite. "I wanted to make sure your first day went well."

Several different versions of the same scolding came to mind. Instead, Fiona set them aside for possible use later. "Thank you, Grace," she said. "I appreciate the effort you've gone to here."

"I hope you like my coffee. My papa says it's the best coffee in Goose Chase, and believe me, he's particular." She set the pot on a folded napkin, then retrieved two cups from the cupboard and filled them. "Be honest. What do you think?"

Fiona blew across the steaming surface of the dark liquid, then gingerly took a sip. It was surely what the coffee in heaven must taste like. To be certain, however, she took a second sip. Then a third.

The dark-haired girl sat wide eyed. "What do you think?"

"I think. . ." Fiona took another taste. "I think this is possibly the best coffee I've had in a long time."

Grace beamed. "You're not just saying that, are you?"

"Well, I don't know," Fiona said. "I'd better take another taste just to be sure. See, there was this coffeehouse in Seattle. . . ." She drained the cup and held it out for more. "Grace, I have to say that you've bested anything I've ever tried. How did you do it?"

"I've had plenty of practice," she said. "See, it's just my papa and me at home, although we do live next to my aunt and uncle and cousins, so I've never felt like I missed much in the way of brothers and sisters. Anyway, my papa works hard, and sometimes he's gone working for the White Pass and Yukon for a week or two at a stretch."

"That must be difficult."

"Oh, I don't like it much, but my aunt's like another mama to me." Grace paused. "She's the only mama I've ever had, actually. Mine only lived long enough to see me born."

Fiona reached across the table to cover Grace's hand with hers. "I'm so sorry," she said softly. "I lost my mama, too."

A fat tear landed on the polished mahogany. "I'm being silly," Grace said. "I got all off track trying to answer your question about coffee. See, one of the times my papa was gone, I asked my aunt if she would teach me to make coffee. Well, when he came back, I figured I was going to make him real happy with what I brewed up."

"How old were you, Grace?"

"Seven going on eight," she said, her grin returning as she swiped at her eyes with a tea napkin.

"And how did he like it?"

"Oh, he praised and praised my coffee. Then he asked me if maybe I would like him to share his secret recipe." She tapped the tabletop with her forefinger. "Wouldn't you know I was thrilled? The next morning we went downstairs together, and he showed me exactly how to make coffee his way."

"Well, he's definitely got a knack for making good coffee. I won't ask your secret, but I sure would like to find out what he does to make it so. . ." She finished off the contents of the second cup and set it back in the saucer. "So very good."

"I'm glad you like it," came a deep and somewhat familiar voice behind her.

Fiona whirled around in her seat, sending the cup and saucer clattering to the floor. Framed by the curtains he held back stood Tucker Smith.

She'd have known him anywhere. Age had touched his face, but in a kind way, and the creases at his temples she hoped to be laugh lines. Somehow knowing Tucker had smiled in the intervening years made her heart soften. The threads of silver in his hair, now that was a surprise.

Fiona rose on shaky legs and gripped the back of the chair. "Tucker?"

"Papa, what are you doing here?"

He looked past Fiona to Grace. "I could ask you the same question, Elizabeth Grace."

"Papa?" *Elizabeth Grace.* Fiona's knees tried to buckle. The girl she'd taken under her wing was the daughter of the woman who. . .

She couldn't complete the thought.

"Sit down, Fiona," he said. "You're swaying, and I have no desire to catch you."

"No," she said as she stiffened her spine and stilled her wobbling knees, "you never really did desire to catch me, did you?"

"Do you two know one another?" Fiona heard the chair legs scrape against the floor, then saw Grace come around to stand beside Tucker. As she wrapped one arm around his waist, she slapped her forehead with the other palm. "Of course. You're the one my daddy's been in love with all these years."

Silence.

Grace clamped her hands over her mouth, flames jumping into her cheeks. "I said that out loud, didn't I? Oh, no." She buried her head in her hands. "Douglas is going to kill me. Neither of us was supposed to know, but we overheard a conversation between his parents. I swear we didn't tell anyone else."

The room was so quiet Fiona could hear her heart pounding in her chest.

"Go home." Tucker ground the words out through clenched jaws. "I will speak to you about this later."

"Yes, Papa. I'm sorry, Dr. Rafferty. I never meant to. . ." Grace looked up at her father, then burst into tears and ran from the room.

A moment later, the front door opened, then slammed shut. For the first time in almost twenty years, Fiona found herself alone with Tucker Smith.

"I'm sorry you had to hear that, Fiona." Tucker stood arrow straight in the doorway. "Where's the doctor?"

"No apology is necessary, Tucker. Your daughter's obviously misunderstood the situation." She paused to give him a chance to dispute the statement, then, to her surprise, felt a bit of disappointment at his silence. "Dr. Killbone is gone," she added. "He left me in charge."

Tucker pinched the bridge of his nose. "For today?"

"No," she said slowly as she avoided Tucker's direct stare, "for six months."

ઝ

Eighteen years fell away, and Tucker stood at a riverbank with the best fisherwoman and the most beautiful—or was it the most exasperating—girl in Alaska. Tucker shook off the memory and concentrated on where he actually was.

He certainly couldn't do anything about his headache now. In the past, Fiona was the cause of headaches, not the cure.

The past.

Like it or not, the past sat right in front of him. There was no more wondering what he'd do when he saw her. What he did was turn around and walk right out the door he came in without saying another word.

He got as far as the sidewalk.

eighteen

The front door slammed shut, and Fiona rose. She took a deep breath and let it out slowly while holding on to the back of the chair for support.

"Six months," she said as she tested her voice. "I can endure anything for six months."

The door opened again, and this time, it shut quietly. *Time to go to work.* "Take a seat, please. I'll be right there."

Fiona picked up her cup and saucer and set them in the sink. Then she washed her hands, drying them on the tea towel. *Thank You, Lord, for giving me the chance to help Dr. Killbone.* She turned around. Tucker Smith stood in the doorway.

"I owe you an apology, Fiona," he said, "and it's eighteen years overdue."

She thought to respond, but Tucker held up his hand to silence her.

"Just let me say this. Once I've said what I have to say, you can tell me to leave you alone, and I will."

A piece of her heart cracked, and she leaned against the counter to remain upright. She dreamed of this moment, this measure of satisfaction over the wrong Tucker had done, for the better part of eighteen years.

When she nodded, he continued. "Good. I assume you'll be keeping the same hours as Doc Killbone."

Another nod.

His expression was unreadable. "Then I'll be here to walk you home when the clinic closes. We can talk then."

The day passed far too quickly, and as the clock edged past four, she found unexpected butterflies in her stomach. She'd just finished giving a new mother advice on a croupy baby when the door flew open. Grace tumbled in with Douglas right behind her.

"Help him," Grace said. "I'm so stupid."

"What in the world are you—"

Grace scooted out of the way to reveal her strapping cousin's pale face. Blood covered the front of his shirt, and his hand seemed to be wrapped in a cloth. Fiona could see stains where the blood tried to seep through.

"What happened?"

"Broken jar. I applied pressure to stop the bleeding, then wrapped it tight and kept it elevated."

Douglas swayed, and Grace slid under his arm to hold him up. Without being told, Grace walked Douglas into the exam room and helped him onto the table. Fiona tagged behind, marveling that the girl knew enough about first aid to assess his ability to move.

"Nerves weren't cut," Grace said. "Looks like you can stitch it."

Fiona cradled her nephew's hand in hers and decided Grace had judged correctly. "Douglas, does it hurt much?"

"No, ma'am," he said. "It stings a bit. It's just that. . ." His face reddened.

Grace leaned toward Fiona. "Blood makes my cousin woozy."

"Does not," Douglas replied.

"Then look at it," Grace said.

"Enough, you two." Fiona placed her hand on Douglas's shoulder. "It's not bad. No glass in the wound. Your cousin took good care of you, and now I'm going to let her help me finish the job."

Douglas looked a bit doubtful. So did Grace.

"Finish the job? What do you mean?"

"Yeah, Aunt Fiona, what do you mean?" Her nephew jerked his hand against his chest, then grimaced. "You're not going to let her sew me up, are you?"

"Grace, would you please tell me how many stitches you think it will take to close the wound?"

Fiona watched the dark-haired girl reach for her cousin's hand and study the wound. "It's only a small cut, but it's deep." She paused. "No more than four, I'd say."

"Well, let's see. Go wash up." She squeezed Douglas's uninjured hand. "Would you like something to take the edge off the pain?"

The young man squared his shoulders. "I'm not a baby, Aunt Fiona. If I'm going to fight in the war, I've got to learn to manage things like this."

Fiona bit back her response while she washed up and gathered supplies. Grace returned and stood by Fiona's side, holding Douglas's elbow while the stitches were sewn. True to Grace's assessment, a fourth would be required to completely close the wound.

Fiona looked at Grace, then addressed Douglas. "You're going to need one more stitch. With your permission, I'm going to let Grace do it."

Douglas didn't even blink. "Sure," he said. "Why not?"

"Grace?" Fiona asked.

The girl met Douglas's gaze before nodding slowly. "I won't hurt you any more than I have to," she told her cousin.

Fiona handed her the tools and exchanged places. "Douglas, speak up if you want me to take over for her."

"That won't be necessary. Go ahead, Grace. Just remember: If you mess up, you'll be taking my shift washing dishes."

"Someone's going to have to take it anyway, goofy," Grace said. "These stitches have to stay dry."

"All right, then." Fiona winked at Grace. "Go right ahead, Dr. Smith. I believe the patient is ready. And I know you are. You're a natural."

With deliberate precision, Grace put the last stitch in place. Fiona showed her how to tie off the thread. The girl bound the wound like a pro, then dropped the instruments into the pan.

"Would you like me to clean these?"

"Grace?"

"Papa?"

Fiona whirled around. Tucker stood behind her. She suppressed a groan. Surely he was furious with her for letting his daughter perform minor surgery.

On closer inspection, however, Fiona could see no anger on his face. Rather, a slow smile dawned.

"Papa, Douglas cut his hand on a broken jar. If I hadn't been next door. . ."

Tucker pressed past Fiona to embrace his daughter. "I'm so proud of you, Lizzie Grace. I watched you sew up Douglas." His voice caught as he met Fiona's stare over his daughter's head. "Fiona's right. You're a natural, sweetheart."

Grace nuzzled against her father's chest. "Do you think so?"

He lifted her chin with his forefinger and planted a kiss on Grace's nose. "I know so." He turned her around to face Fiona. "I wonder, Dr. Rafferty, do you think my daughter might benefit from medical school training?"

Fiona fought to control her smile. "Why, yes, Mr. Smith. I think your daughter shows great potential. May I have your permission to speak to my former professor at the medical college in Oregon on her behalf?"

"Oh, yes, please do," Tucker said.

Grace danced a jig, then regained her composure. "Thank you, Papa," she said. "I promise to make you proud."

Tucker embraced his daughter once more. "I'm already proud, Lizzie Grace."

"I'm so happy, I'm going to ignore the fact that you just called me Lizzie Grace." She addressed Douglas. "You seem awfully happy." Grace nudged his shoulder. "Are you trying to get rid of me?"

"No." Douglas studied his bandaged hand before meeting

his cousin's gaze. "But you and I have looked after one another ever since I can remember. If you're not going to war, I don't have to go, either."

Tucker shook his head. "You mean you were only joining up because Grace was?"

Douglas nodded. "Yes, sir. I knew she wanted to join those Canadian nurses, so I figured I could put in for a duty in the same place they sent her and keep an eye on things."

"That's very noble of you, Douglas." Fiona smiled. "Your parents have done a wonderful job of raising you."

The young man shrugged. "I don't know about all that, Aunt Fiona. Most of the time, she's just a little tagalong, but I figure we're family, and we ought to look out for one another."

"Douglas, I'm going to ignore that first comment," Grace said. "I'm sure you're delirious from the pain." She jabbed his shoulder with her elbow, and he gave a playful yelp. "Dr. Rafferty, I believe the patient needs to go home now. Would you like me to wash those instruments before I walk the big oaf home?"

"No, darling, I think I can handle it."

"Fiona," Tucker said, "I believe you and I have plans. Perhaps my daughter should clean up while you and I go for a walk. Should she lock up when she's done?"

Flustered, Fiona could only nod and scurry after her hat and handbag. A moment later, she found herself walking down Third Street beside Tucker Smith.

She took a deep breath of clean, crisp evening air. "It's a good thing you're doing for your daughter, Tucker."

He blew out a long breath. "An hour ago, I would have said something completely different." He paused. "But watching her in there with you, well, I could see it was something the Lord meant her to do."

Fiona stepped around a patch of mud. "I agree."

"Something else." Tucker sighed. "Much as I hate to admit

it, I was wrong about you, Fiona."

She gave him a sideways look. "Oh?"

"All those years," he said slowly, "I consoled myself by thinking that you were probably as unhappy as I was. Before you judge me, you ought to know that I believed you were made to be a wife and not a doctor."

Pausing at the corner, they let a motorcar and two horses pass before crossing the street. "And?" she finally said.

"And now I know you couldn't be unhappy, not when you are so obviously suited to this line of work."

Fiona stopped on the sidewalk in front of her house. "Work isn't everything, Tucker."

Her statement seemed to surprise him. She leaned against the Ford and studied him while she tried to decide how much of the truth to tell him.

"Should you be doing that?" Tucker gestured toward the car. "I mean, the owner might not cotton to having you lean on it."

"I assure you the owner is perfectly fine with me touching it." Laughing, Fiona opened the car door. "Would you like to go for a ride?"

Tucker took two steps back. "You own this motorcar?"

She patted the door. "I do."

"I'm assuming it's no small coincidence that I was nearly killed by a woman driving a vehicle that looked very much like this one." He walked in a circle completely around the car. "Ma'am, do you own a black hat with a large feather?" He slapped his knee. "Of course, you do. If I remember correctly, you always did like odd hats." He glanced down at her shoes. "And you had a weakness for fancy footwear, too."

They shared a laugh; then Tucker grew solemn. "Close the door, Fiona. I need to say what I came to say, and I can't do it in that contraption."

"All right." She closed the door. "Merry sent me home with leftovers, and there's always coffee at my house."

Tucker looked up and nodded. "Coffee will do."

৯

Tucker sipped at his coffee and tried to decide where to start. The beginning sounded about right, so he took a deep breath and let it out slowly while Fiona settled across the kitchen table from him.

"Once I get to talking," he said, "I'd appreciate it if you'd let me finish. Then you can send me packing, if that's what you want." When she nodded, he continued. "It all started when Mama died. Papa never was the same. He left Meredith and me to ourselves most of the time, and one day he just didn't come home. The sheriff came to tell us he'd been shot by a man he owed money to."

His throat felt like cotton, so he gulped the coffee and continued before he lost his nerve. "Turns out he owed just about everyone in the county. Only way I knew to take care of things was to bring Merry to Uncle Darian's place and then head for Alaska to make enough to pay everyone back. Turns out my sister had other plans. Merry refused to be left behind, and that's how both of us ended up in Alaska."

Fiona smiled. "That sounds like Merry."

"Yes, well, when I left Texas, I knew I couldn't go back." He lifted his gaze to meet Fiona's. "I was engaged at the time. To Elizabeth." He paused to take another sip of liquid courage. "I spoke to her father, and he agreed it was best that we call off the wedding. Elizabeth was grateful for being spared the humiliation of marrying into my family."

"I'm sorry, Tucker. That must have been very difficult."

He nodded. "Honestly, I didn't blame her, but I found after a while I didn't miss her, either. Then came Ian and the baby, and Braden married Amy. Well, I started feeling like I was the odd man out. Merry knew this and took it upon herself to write Elizabeth. By that time, I had used my share of the inheritance from Uncle Darian's estate to pay the debts. That's where I was going when I ran into you aboard that trawler."

"Oh?"

"I always knew you weren't intending to stay in Goose Chase. You said so that day at the docks." He wrapped his hand around the delicate cup and let the warmth seep into his palm. "I didn't like you much at first," he said with a laugh. "I thought you were a little. . .how should I say this? Prissy."

"Me? Prissy?"

"Obviously you've forgotten the fancy hat and shoes you wore on that first trip back to town."

"Guilty," she said with a grin.

"Anyway, let's just say you grew on me until those fishing trips got to be the highlight of my week. No one was as surprised as me when I figured out I'd fallen in love with you. The day I asked you to marry me, I thought I was free and clear to do so."

His heart ripped in half when he saw that Fiona had begun to cry. "Do you want me to stop?" She shook her head, so he continued. "I know Merry thought she was doing the right thing in contacting Elizabeth. Do you understand why I married her, Fiona?"

"I'm not sure," she said softly. "I figured you still loved her."

Tucker reached across the table to grasp Fiona's wrist. "No, I loved you. I don't think I ever stopped loving you." He released her and continued. "It became apparent the night I married Elizabeth why she was so quick to head to Alaska when she got Merry's letter."

Fiona studied the tabletop. "I don't think I need to hear this."

"Look at me, Fiona." When she complied, he continued. "She was with child. Three months gone with a baby that belonged to some cowboy. When the rogue refused to marry her, she came after me." Tucker paused. "After she had Grace, Elizabeth ran off to meet him. Years later, her death certificate arrived."

The color drained from Fiona's face. "Then Grace is not—"

"Not my natural daughter?" He shook his head. "No, but you're the only one I've ever admitted that to. I'm sure Merry realizes it, but she would never say anything. She was still nursing Douglas when Grace came along, so those two were raised together like twins."

"Like you and Merry."

"I never thought of that, but you're right." He ran his hands through his hair and shored up his courage with more coffee. "I know now that I tried to take back up with you too soon, and I'm sorry if I made things difficult for you by writing those letters. I just wonder now if the Lord has given us another chance. . .if maybe now that we're in our twilight years, it's finally our time."

"Hey, speak for yourself, Tucker. I'm still young." She worried with the coffee cup. "But maybe you're right."

Tucker felt like a weight had been removed from his shoulders—and his heart. "I've been waiting eighteen years to tell you that."

Fiona smiled. "And I've been waiting eighteen years to hear it."

"Sitting here and looking at you now, well, it's like all those years never happened. I'm almost afraid to ruin things by telling you this, but I'm still as much in love with you today as I was the day you left."

She rose and walked to the coffeepot, and for a minute Tucker felt he'd said too much. He was about to backpedal when Fiona turned around and smiled.

nineteen

"All I know is, he and Ian were locked away in the front parlor for nearly half an hour last night," Meredith said. "You and I both know those two don't have that much to talk about." She paused. "Unless he's asking for your hand in marriage."

Fiona fussed with the ribbons on her hat and tried not to let Meredith's enthusiasm get her hopes up. "True, we have been getting along famously," Fiona admitted, "but marriage? He hasn't given so much as a hint."

Meredith looked undaunted. "I know my brother, and he's up to something. You two have been inseparable for the past month. I don't think he's going to hold off much longer."

"Yes, he is, actually." She leaned conspiratorially toward Meredith. "He's asked me to teach him to drive."

"No!"

"Yes. I'm taking him for a driving lesson today." Fiona touched her sister-in-law's arm. "Please don't say a word. I'm sure it's not easy for a man with Tucker's ego to have to learn anything from a woman."

"Then why bother?" Meredith snapped her fingers. "Of course. You own an automobile, and if he's going to be your husband, he's not going to sit still for his wife driving him around. See, I told you he's about to pop the question."

"Hush, here he comes." Fiona waved at Tucker, then gave her sister-in-law a kiss on the cheek.

"I want all the details," Meredith whispered.

❧

"You've got to be joking." Tucker stared down the length of Broadway, both hands on the steering wheel. "You expect me to learn how to drive by going down the middle of the street?"

"There's nothing on this end of Broadway but empty land. By the time you get way down there, you'll be a natural at driving."

"You make it sound simple."

Fiona nodded. "You're a smart man, and we've been over this a dozen times. It's only a motorcar, Tucker. Surely a man who's worked on the railroad all these years can handle a simple Ford."

His pride trampled, Tucker decided he must do this. The engine purred and rumbled, and the steering wheel vibrated under his fingers. He reached for the stick and followed Fiona's directions. The car lurched forward and promptly died.

To her credit, Fiona didn't laugh. Rather, she gently pointed him in the right direction, and eventually, she managed to get the car rolling forward at a consistent speed.

"Hey, look," he said when he could manage to remain calm, "I'm driving." Tucker began to think about the real reason for this drive, and he pressed a bit harder on the pedal that made the car go. "This isn't hard at all."

"Tucker, slow down."

He looked over at Fiona. "Worried?"

"Tucker!"

Turning his attention to the road, he managed to miss a pair of wagons looming in his path. "How do I turn this thing?"

When she showed him, he tried it at the next opportunity. The vehicle promptly died.

"How about we go somewhere safer?" she offered. "Somewhere with fewer people."

Tucker smiled. "I know exactly the road." He saw it up ahead and turned right without having to start the Ford again. The vehicle sputtered and lurched but smoothed out as it headed over the hill.

Then came the part he wasn't prepared for: downhill.

The Ford picked up speed. "How do I stop this thing?"

"The brake, Tucker!" Fiona shouted as trees whizzed by. "Hit the brake!"

But instead of the brake, Tucker hit the curb and managed a quick left-hand turn that caused the Ford to slide sideways. They rode like that for a full block before Tucker regained control. He straightened the automobile just in time to run up into the yard of the parsonage.

"Get back on the road, Tucker!" she called. "The church is up ahead!"

"I know," he said as he found the brake and brought the Ford to a screeching halt inches from the back wall of the church. He jumped out and ran around to help a shaking Fiona out of the Ford.

"I was going to do this in a much grander manner, but considering we're in the right place for it, will you marry me, Fiona?"

"Marry you?" She leaned against the Ford, and Tucker hoped the flush in her cheeks was excitement at his proposal rather than something to do with their wild ride.

"Say yes, Fiona. We'd like to come out and congratulate the bride and groom." Braden called from around the corner of the church. "Is it safe to come out now, or is Tucker still driving?"

The rest of the Rafferty clan came pouring out of the church, surrounding them. Grace pressed forward to wrap her arms around Fiona before addressing her father.

"I hope you said it like we practiced last night." She turned to Fiona. "How did he do?"

Fiona smiled. "I can honestly say his was the most memorable proposal I've ever had."

"So," Amy said, "he asked, but you didn't tell us what the answer was."

Tucker wrapped his arms around the most beautiful woman in Alaska—or was she the most exasperating? "That's right,

Fiona. You haven't given me your answer. If you don't want to go into the church and marry me, I can always drive you home."

❧

The wedding took place in the little chapel beside the tall trees with Grace as Fiona's attendant and both brothers walking her down the aisle. Meredith, Amy, and Grace had managed to find Fiona a lovely dress and had even acquired an exquisite hat and the most lovely pair of bridal shoes a girl could wear.

Fiona floated through the ceremony, half expecting to wake up from the lovely dream. While Braden drove the car back to Fiona's place, Tucker and Fiona were escorted by wagon to a lovely cabin on the other side of the hills from Goose Chase for a long-delayed honeymoon.

All winter, the women planned Grace's trip to medical school in Oregon. The night before Grace was to leave, Fiona slipped into her room with a long list of names of friends and colleagues for the girl to contact once she got settled at the school.

"And no matter what," Fiona said, "you're to return home for Christmas."

"Maybe you and Papa should come to Oregon for Christmas," she said. "You know I don't plan to be there any longer than it takes for me to become a doctor."

"Yes, dear, and I'd like to talk to you about that."

Later that night, Fiona climbed under the thick stack of quilts to snuggle against her husband. "Are you asleep?" she whispered.

Tucker turned to gather Fiona in his arms. "No, I'm just lying here wondering how we're going to fill all the empty hours we'll have once Grace leaves."

Fiona smiled and leaned up on one elbow. "Oh, I don't think that will be a problem, Tucker. A little bird tells me that we're going to be plenty busy come spring."

"Spring?" Even in the dim light, Fiona could see Tucker's

broad grin. "Fiona? You're not. Are you?"

"Yes," she whispered. "Isn't God good?"

"Oh, yes," he said as he kissed her soundly. To her surprise, Tucker pulled away. "But if you're indisposed, who will be the doctor around here?"

It was Fiona's turn to smile. "Doc Killbone said he'd be sending a replacement in six months. I'm sure he will be willing to stay until Grace returns."

"Grace?" He shook his head. "I don't understand."

"She told me tonight that she intends to return to Goose Chase and practice medicine. That means your daughter will be home in a few years." Fiona stole a kiss from her surprised husband. "Are you happy, Tucker Smith?"

He answered, but not with words.

A Letter To Our Readers

Dear Reader:

In order that we might better contribute to your reading enjoyment, we would appreciate your taking a few minutes to respond to the following questions. We welcome your comments and read each form and letter we receive. When completed, please return to the following:

Fiction Editor
Heartsong Presents
PO Box 719
Uhrichsville, Ohio 44683

1. Did you enjoy reading *Golden Twilight* by Kathleen Y'Barbo?
   ❏ Very much! I would like to see more books by this author!
   ❏ Moderately. I would have enjoyed it more if

   _____

   _____

   _____

2. Are you a member of **Heartsong Presents**? ❏ Yes ❏ No
   If no, where did you purchase this book? _____

   _____

3. How would you rate, on a scale from 1 (poor) to 5 (superior), the cover design? _____

4. On a scale from 1 (poor) to 10 (superior), please rate the following elements.

   ____ Heroine   ____ Plot
   ____ Hero   ____ Inspirational theme
   ____ Setting   ____ Secondary characters

5. These characters were special because? _____

_____

_____

6. How has this book inspired your life? _____

_____

_____

7. What settings would you like to see covered in future
   Heartsong Presents books? _____

_____

_____

8. What are some inspirational themes you would like to see
   treated in future books? _____

_____

_____

9. Would you be interested in reading other **Heartsong
   Presents** titles? ❏ Yes ❏ No

10. Please check your age range:

    ❏ Under 18   ❏ 18-24
    ❏ 25-34   ❏ 35-45
    ❏ 46-55   ❏ Over 55

Name _____

Occupation _____

Address _____

City, State, Zip _____

Louisiana
BRIDES

3 stories in 1

Three young women's hearts are rooted in the Bayou.

Devoted to their Louisiana bayou homes, three women find love while being pulled from their Cajun country.

Stories include: *Bayou Fever*, *Bayou Beginnings*, and *Bayou Secrets* by author Kathleen Y'Barbo.

Historical, paperback, 368 pages, 5³⁄₁₆" x 8"
